AF225545

Eric Stiles has everything to lose and no matter how hard he fights, he can feel his life slipping away.

Rebecca Gailen thinks that the love of her life is dead and only the vigor of revenge keeps her fighting to survive.

When a secret reveals more than anyone expected, it changes Eric and Rebecca's lives forever. The devastating truth puts the couple at odds. Can they overcome their clashing conclusions and learn to trust each other again? Or will they let it rip them apart?

The unauthorized reproduction or distribution of this copyrighted work is illegal. Criminal copyright infringement, including infringement without monetary gain, is investigated by the FBI and is punishable by up to 5 years in federal prison and a fine of $250,000.

This book is a work of fiction. Names, characters, places, and incidents either are products of the author's imagination or are used fictitiously. Any resemblance to actual events or locales or persons, living or dead, is entirely coincidental.

Jaded Promises
Copyright © 2019 Amy Romine
ISBN: 978-1-4874-2468-8
Cover art by Martine Jardin

All rights reserved. Except for use in any review, the reproduction or utilization of this work in whole or in part in any form by any electronic, mechanical or other means, now known or hereafter invented, is forbidden without the written permission of the publisher.

Published by eXtasy Books Inc or
Devine Destinies, an imprint of eXtasy Books Inc

Look for us online at:
www.eXtasybooks.com or www.devinedestinies.com

Jaded Promises
Trust Me, Book 3

By

Amy Romine

Dedication

My husband, Robert, our three children and my extended family. To Brenda (my Donna), Sean, the man with the knowledge, and finally my professional family whose constant support will never be forgotten.

CHAPTER ONE

The air seemed to disappear as his arm dropped. Eric had to remind himself how to breathe. He went through the motions, his brain signaled his lungs to expand and yet still nothing happened. The absence of oxygen started to cloud his vision. He ordered his legs to move. A moment later, he stepped into the sunshine. The hot desert breeze mocked him as it curled around his neck.

His chest moved and his mind seemed to reconnect with his body. He closed his eyes, his heart processing the information from Dr. Raines before tucking it away.

Charlie pulled up and they headed out to the first address on the list of possible locations Marco Valnes could be holding Rebecca and Lucy. Along with Jorge's location, they also made a list of every location recently deserted or sold.

Eric's mind spun with the passing scenery, the clock in his brain continuing to tick. The sun rose, bringing with it the harsh light of reality. A new day without Rebecca and his heart thudded painfully in his ears. It seemed easier in the dark of the night. The blackness cushioned the raging of his heart, but now the day dawned and she was still missing.

His thoughts turned dark and he rejected them. *No. I am going to find her.*

"Which way?"

Charlie's voice pulled Eric out of his head.

"Eric?"

He did his best to push the helplessness away, shove it down and lock it in a steel trap for another time. "Left."

Gulping back the pressure that surrounded his heart before, he turned his attention to the road ahead.

"Is that it?"

"Yeah."

Charlie pulled off the road and parked the truck before reaching beneath the seat to grab Eric's spare weapon.

"Ready?"

Charlie nodded and the pair stepped out of the truck and split up. He took the back and Eric the front.

Eric swerved through the maze of dead trees and scattered brush before he reached the front porch and climbed the steps. The place looked deserted, but there was no sense in taking any risks.

"Las Vegas Police, anybody home?"

With no response, Eric tried the door. It turned in his hand and opened without effort. He quickly cleared the door, searching each room, he found the house abandoned.

"Charlie!"

"Clear!" his brother called from the back of the house.

He pushed the air out of his lungs, heard his brother's footsteps and holstered his weapon. They investigated the entire house, top to bottom. His mind throbbed with agonizing weight, the blackness of despair hovered just a few breaths away. "This place is deserted. There hasn't been anyone here in a while."

"You're sure?" Charlie met him on the porch.

"Yeah, I'm sure. Why, did you find something?"

"No."

Eric shook his head as he took one last look. Charlie followed behind and they got into the truck, looking up the second address.

"The next address is outside Indian Springs," Eric said as Charlie pulled onto the road. Eric dialed Lug, who was heading the search from the police station, and got his voicemail. His focus went to the scenery, consciously keeping himself centered and steady.

His phone buzzed and he answered. "Detective Stiles."

"Stiles," Lug said. "They found one of the girls."

"Where?"

"Crystal Springs PD."

They rushed into the station, bursting through the doors and searching the small office before them. Eric's gaze stopped as he saw mouse brown hair.

"Is that Lucy?" Rebecca's baby sister sat on a couch toward the back of the room.

"Yes," he pulled back the swing of disappointment that hit his chest.

She rose, her eyes wide with emotion. "Eric?"

"Lucy." She stepped toward him and he pulled her into a hug. "Are you okay?"

"I . . . I think so."

He sat her down on the couch next to him. "Can you tell me what happened?"

Charlie took a seat across from them.

She explained how everything played out.

Eric did his best to keep his emotions at bay. He tried to remain focused as she described the abuse and torture Marco forced them to endure at the house they just left.

"How did you get away?"

"Marco took us to a meeting. He needed Rebecca to do an exchange."

"What kind of exchange?"

"I don't know. There were two silver briefcases, but I never saw what was in them."

"So Marco had Rebecca do the exchange?"

"Yes, she did the exchange and came back to the SUV."

Her knees shook against the couch. "I remember Marco's phone rang and she looked at me. I could tell she was planning something. She stepped forward and swung the metal case at Marco's head. She screamed for me to run so I did . . . I thought she was behind me . . ."

"It's okay, Lucy, take your time," Charlie moved, taking the seat next to her.

"It was dark, I couldn't see anything. I just ran. I don't know how far away I was, but I heard what sounded like popping. "Her eyes shifted down to her hands. "I think they . . . shot at us . . . when I didn't see her, I wanted to go back . . . I didn't want to leave her there. Eric . . . I didn't know what . . ."She crumbled into a shivering ball of tears.

Eric wrapped his arm around her in comfort. He looked at Charlie in hesitation, his mind lurching in fear. "You got away and we found you. You're safe. That's all that matters."

"Lucy, do you have any idea where Marco was planning to go or where he might be headed?" Charlie said, his hand resting on her shoulder.

"I don't know."

"Do you have any idea about what is so special about the locket?"

"We think that there's something hidden in your mother's locket. Do you know anything about that?" Eric's body became restless and he stood.

"I knew that Marco had something hidden in the locket, but I never knew what," she shook her head. "Marco did say that he needed it. He seemed really desperate."

"Needed it for what?"

"I don't know. I'm so sorry. This is all my fault and now she's . . ."Her eyes welled with tears, cursing the moment she met Marco Valnes and unleashed him into their lives. "Eric, you have to find her. Please, I know that this is all my fault. I'm begging you, please. You have to find my sister."

"We're going to find her, I promise." Eric's phone buzzed against his hip. He rose to answer it and Charlie stayed with Lucy. Looking at the screen he recognized it, "Adam, talk to me."

"They may have found the house," Adam said. "I am sending the address to your phone. "The Sheriff is on sight."

"We're on our way."

"Eric, look," Charlie said half an hour later as they saw activity ahead of them. A house surrounded by police. Charlie pulled up alongside. Before the truck stopped, Eric jumped out, running to the scene.

"Detective Stiles," someone called and he raced toward the uniformed officer.

"Tell me you know where they went . . ."

"No."

Eric's heart dropped into his stomach.

"But we're pretty sure they were here."

"Why?" Charlie asked, joining them.

"We found this," he handed Eric a small plastic bag containing a piece of fabric wrapped in several strands of deep red hair.

"Where?"

"The basement," he motioned inside before nodding that it was okay for him to go in.

Eric stepped through the front door, feeling Charlie behind him. He took a breath, following the hallway to the back of the house. A few random officers milled about as he passed. They came to a heavy wooden door. It was cracked open and Eric pushed it aside. It wailed in protest and he stepped into the darkness.

The stairs creaked with each step he took into the dimness below. The humid musty area was cold and damp. He swallowed hard. Gray concrete, unfinished jagged walls and dust surrounded them. A chill raked up his spine.

"We found it over there," the same officer descended the stairs behind them. The beam of his flashlight landed to the right of where they stood.

Eric reached for a flashlight and his gaze landed on Charlie who scanned the room. An officer offered his and Eric stepped toward the area. His hand brushed against the cold concrete, but his mind still refused to accept it.

Not here . . . not like this . . .

Eric's gaze fell on a spatter of blood and his chest flooded with an unrecognized pain.

She was here.

Unable to push the image away, he could see her trapped in the dismal space of the basement. All the air left the room and his entire body clenched at the suffocation. He ascended the stairs into the sunlit area. His lungs took in the stale air. He fought for control. He mindlessly entered one of the side rooms, feeling himself begin to unhinge.

They didn't find her, which means she's still . . .

Keep it together, Stiles . . . falling apart isn't going to help anyone.

The sewn seam around his emotions threatened to tear and he couldn't move. The paralyzing agony that spiked from the core of his body was relentless. He fought back in vain. He knew it wouldn't stop until she was in his arms, safe.

"Eric, what's going on?"

Eric shifted, wiping an unexpected wetness from his eyes. He leaned against the wall, facing his brother. Pure disbelief staring back at him. It was apparent that he'd changed into something his brother didn't recognize.

"I've never seen you like this."

"Yeah?"

"Yeah, you never . . ."

"Yeah well, things change."

Eric exited the room and pushed through the front door, hearing Charlie just behind him.

"Since when?"

"You still don't get it, do you?"

"What are you talking about?"

"Have you really convinced yourself that all of this . . . what happened, was just some kind of joke?" Eric asked as he stopped and turned to face Charlie. "That Rebecca and I lied and hid our feelings from you because we thought it was fun?"

"I don't know what the hell you meant to do and to be honest, I don't really care."

"Charlie . . . whether or not you choose to believe, Rebecca and I didn't expect to get involved, we tried to walk away from our feelings, but we couldn't."

Charlie's eyes diverted in anger.

"Jesus, Charlie, she went through hell and all she could think about was how she couldn't hurt you!"

"So once again this is my fault!"

"No . . . I am just . . ." Eric tried to keep his emotions in check. "As your brother, your friend, I tried to forget about . . . everything. But that night. That first night in Dallas, everything changed. Rebecca and I did everything we could to ignore it, make the feelings disappear, but they didn't. They only got stronger . . . can you try to understand that?"

"You really expect me to —"

"I expect you to believe that I tried! I expect you to realize that what happed between Rebecca and I had nothing to do with you. To remember that until that moment, I've never betrayed you."

"So, because you've always tried to be the good big brother you want me to be okay with this? To just accept you stealing the woman I love away from me and move on?"

"Yes."

"Why?"

"Because you're my brother and I need you to." Eric's eyes watered despite his continued battle against it. "Charlie, I'm in love with her."

"I loved her, too!"

"Okay, Charlie," Eric clenched his jaw. "Where did you see things heading with her? Let's say we never met. What then?"

"I don't know. I never got the chance, thanks to you!"

"That's the difference!" Eric pushed back in frustration. "Six weeks ago and the two months before that, hell even in Dallas. I knew this was different. I knew she changed everything. Even when she left without a word and I didn't even know her name, I couldn't get her out of my head! I look at her and see everything I never knew I wanted. She's woken up this person inside me that I didn't even know was there! The one who wants a house and a family. The person who needs to see her every morning and hold her every night, because when I don't, something is missing and the world doesn't make sense."

"Eric—"

"The difference is that the moment I met her, she became my whole world," he struggled to keep his furious heart under control. "I know that you loved her. That was one of the reasons I stayed away as long as I did. It might not seem like much, but . . . she needed me and I couldn't turn my back anymore. Now she's gone and I can't . . . If we don't . . . if I can't find her . . ."

"We're going to find her, Eric."

Eric saw the first glimpse of understanding in his brother's eyes. His phone beeped with a message from Lug to call. "Lugow, what's up?"

"We got a break."

"What've you got?" Eric's heart leapt in his chest while he glanced at Charlie.

"I have a cell call to 911 with an SOS. We're working on a location now."

"Can you send it over?"

"No."

"Why?"

"Eric, just . . ."

"Tech is tracking the line?"

"Yeah, I am conferencing Carl in now."

"Tech Ops, this is Carl."

"Carl, save my life."

"Stiles, we're almost there."

"How close are you?"

"We're within 100 miles."

"That's not close enough, Carl."

"I know. I'm working on it."

"Call me as soon as you have an address. We're going to need three teams. Call Narcotics and make sure they're ready to move as soon as we get a location. Lugow?"

"Yeah?"

"Is Adam around?"

"Yeah, hang on."

"Eric . . ."

"I want to hear it," is all he needed to say and Adam knew what he was talking about.

"You don't . . ."

"Adam, send it," his blood pressure rising.

"It's on its way."

Eric hung up and headed toward the truck.

"Where are we headed?"

"Not sure, south, I think."

"You think?"

"Yeah," Eric started the truck, waited for Charlie to get in and pulled out. His chest burned in anticipation of what he was going to hear. His phone vibrated and he looked down at the audio file. He took a breath, readied himself and hit play.

There was a soft breath on her neck while light fingers touched her hair.

Eric . . .

A steady ache rose from her body, her conscious lifting into an explosion of color. Rebecca's eyes opened as she was yanked upward and found herself inches from Marco's face. His stale breath tugged at the rising nausea in her throat.

"Good morning, sleeping beauty."

She grasped at the wall to steady herself until her legs caught up.

"Time to go."

"What are you talking about?"

"Well despite your hesitation, your earlier performance sealed your fate." He gave her a wide smile and her strength began to return. "I think you'll be very happy where you're going. It's not that unlike Vegas, although you may experience a little culture shock. I'm sure you'll adapt—"

"I'm not going anywhere."

"Now you see? Here I am trying to make this transition as easy as possible for you. However, as usual, you have to go and complicate things by being difficult. I'd think that you would've learned to treat me with a little more respect by now, Rebecca."

She knew what was coming. Despite her attempt to deflect the blow, her body wasn't fast enough. The grayness faded her vision as she hit the concrete. Rebecca pushed herself up on one arm as she heard him bark at his thugs.

The thugs unchained her manacles, lifted her off the floor and led her from her cell. She attempted to walk but ended up tripping over her own feet. They took her down the hallway and pushed her into the familiar bedroom.

The door closed. She leaned heavily against the wall, her body sluggish and aching. Once again, she found clothing on the bed, a flimsy burgundy dress and strap high heels. Her limbs still not responding to her commands, she reached for the side of the bed, grasping it tightly. She tried to keep her balance as she moved across the room.

With a deep breath, she grabbed the dress and reached for the door of the bathroom. A sudden wave of nausea overwhelmed her as she twisted the knob. Her stomach clenched and she darted for the toilet where she emptied out the contents of her stomach. Given she hadn't recently eaten, there wasn't much in there. She choked on the stomach acid that came instead, begging her body to stop.

Her head rested against her arm. Her entire body pulsed in agony. She closed her eyes, desperately wanting to drift off into the warmth of sleep. She could feel his arms around her.

He's gone. You saw the photo.

You're going on a trip.

They're moving you, play your cards right and you might be able to get out of here.

Okay, Beccs, time to man up . . . you can't let him win.

Rebecca lifted herself off the floor, turned on the shower and stepped out of the black cocktail dress. She remembered her trick with the cell phone and wondered if anyone got the message. Was it still in the flower arrangement? Had he found it? Maybe the cavalry was on the way. How long would it take them to find her? How long had she been asleep?

Her mind finally woke up and stepping into the shower, her thoughts spun with what to do next. Marco said she was going on a trip. Should she try for an escape during the trip or should she stall? The phone was here and she figured they would find some way to track it, right? That would take time and if she was gone when they arrived, there was no way to tell them where she'd gone.

Before she had a chance to decide anything, pain cut her in half and she fell to her knees. She clutched her abdomen, her body trembling uncontrolled. Doubled up on the floor of the shower, she silently wished it away. The spasm pushed her strength to a breaking point and she fought for control.

What the hell is wrong with me?

She planted her hands against the tile of the wall, waiting for the spell to pass.

Come on, Beccs, you need to pull it together.
You can't lose it yet. You have to keep going.
He would want you to keep going.
You can do this . . . just breathe . . .

The pain subsided, her sight cleared and she stepped out of the shower. Unable to stop trembling, she dried herself off and pulled on the dress. She looked at her reflection in the mirror and couldn't help but sigh. The dress was too thin, too short and too . . .

Whatever.

Too exhausted to care, she twisted toward the counter. Her abdomen tightened and she stopped in caution. Rebecca waited for it to pass, suspended just above agony. Her heart thumped against her chest in panic and she ordered her body to relax.

Stop it . . . stop it . . .

Rebecca pushed the fear into the back of her mind as she focused on her hair and makeup. By the time she finished, her body had settled. She smoothed the dress over her hips and walked out of the bathroom.

His mind frantic, he couldn't drive fast enough to suppress the intense anxiety bubbling beneath his skin. The recording was burned into his mind. The sounds of her crying and struggling as they did God only knew what. He did his best to push it away.

He knew where she was, he just needed to get to her. Once that happened, his heart would stop racing. His chest would calm and he would be able to breathe again.

I just need to get to her.

His mind began to list all of the things that could go wrong.

He hovered just above his own awareness. The pieces of rational thought broke away, his mind corralling around one single storm. Rational thought was muffled in a drunken haze, induced by overwhelming terror. He continued to drive, unconsciously counting the seconds without her.

"Eric."

Her screams echoed in his mind.

I have to remain in control.

He kept the panic and the fury under his belt. Trapped behind his stomach, knowing that it would be energy wasted.

"Eric," his brother's voice echoed in Eric's head, but he continued to drive.

He could feel it unravel, fear and desperation inching into his heart. A dagger slowly piercing him as each moment was lost. Eric pulled off the road and hit the brakes. He leapt out of the truck. His mind spinning, he walked, forcing air into his lungs.

A door slammed. "Eric!"

He didn't know how to stop his mind's rapid descent into blinding paralyzing fear. He didn't know how to take it back and shut it down.

"Stop," Charlie called.

He continued to ignore him.

"Eric, stop!"

His back hit the side of the truck. Charlie pinned him against it.

"What?"

"Look at me!"

"Get off!"

"Tell me what's going on."

"Charlie, *stop*!" his brother's face settled in determination. It was too much.

"No, not until you tell me what the hell's going on!"

For the first time, it was too much.

"She's pregnant!"

The reality of uttering it aloud was so much worse than he imagined. Charlie's hold on him loosened. His body sagged as the unbridled panic poured out of him.

"What?"

Eric continued to battle with himself, his eyes heating with the threat of tears. "Rebecca's pregnant." The fuel that had kept him going suddenly depleted.

"How do you . . ."

"She had an appointment with Dr. Raines. A follow-up." He pushed his hand over his scalp. "He heard what happened on the news and he called me."

"When did he call you?" Charlie crouched in front of him.

"Right after we talked to Reynolds," Eric said, recalling his power struggle for information with the psychotic monster.

"Does Rebecca know?"

"I don't think so." Unable to dam the emotions in his chest, the question stabbed at him. His hands rubbed over his face, struggling to push it back. "He said she's only about six weeks along."

"Wow . . . I don't—"

"I did this."

"Did what?"

"I could've stopped this . . ."

"What are you talking about?"

"I promised her this was over. She asked me to tell her the truth. I said she didn't have anything to be scared of—"

"Eric, there's no—"

"I was supposed to be there with her!" His anger burst forth. "I was supposed to go with her to meet Lucy."

"There was no way for you to know what was going to happen. You can't second guess yourself now."

"Yes, I can. Maybe I should! If I would've stopped focusing so hard on making a pointless collar, I would've been at the hospital. I could've stopped it and she would be safe!"

"Eric—"

"I say I love her and yet I can't even find her when she needs me the most! We've been running around chasing geese when she could be . . ." he looked away from Charlie, unable to continue the thought aloud.

"All right, enough," Charlie said. "You're not allowed to doubt whether or not you should or do love her!"

"Charlie . . ."

"Shut up. Back at the house, when you said that I didn't get it," regret shone in his eyes. "That day, when I walked into the hospital room . . . . .I saw the way she clung to you and I hated you. Because that was supposed to be me! You said you loved her and I refused to believe it. Unable to think that you could possibly love her as much as I did."

"That's not—"

"Shut up. I know she didn't choose you over me, Eric. I realized you don't get to choose. It just happens. You were meant to be together. I'm sorry if I ever got in the way or jeopardized what you found with Rebecca. I want you to be happy, Eric."

"It all happened so fast . . . suddenly I wanted all of these things I never knew I wanted, because of her." Tormented frustration stole the strength of his body. "When you told me she was gone, I coped. Beccs can handle herself, she's tough. I knew she would be okay until I found her, but now . . ."

"It's changed."

"Charlie," his anxiety spilled over his words. "She doesn't know . . . what if something happens? She's . . . what if I can't get to her. I . . . I can't lose her, Charlie . . . I can't . . ."

"She's strong, Eric. You have to know your baby is strong. He or she has the Stiles will and Rebecca's fire," Charlie said in reassurance as he put a hand on his brother's shoulder. "We're going to find her and as soon as you see her, all of this crap is going to disappear."

Eric took a breath and his phone buzzed. "Talk to me."

They both got back in the truck.

"I have the coordinates. They're coming over to you now. Lug wanted me to tell you that he's dispatched Narcotics and the Boulder City Sheriff.

"How far out are they?"

"Five, maybe ten minutes. Good luck."

Eric ended the call and pulled up the coordinates. He transferred them over into the GPS before handing the phone to Charlie. "Here are the coordinates, once it loads tell me how far out we are."

"Ten miles west."

Eric took a breath. "Grab the vests from the back seat." He focused on keeping the truck at max speed.

They were so close.

"Here, turn left!"

There was a knock on the door. She quickly pulled on the shoes and took a breath before she opened the door. The thug looked her over with a grin. He grabbed her arm, escorting her from the room.

"Too bad we had so little time together. I think I would've enjoyed having you as a toy for a while."

Marco appeared in the hallway in front of them. He stepped into her space, his hands brushing through her hair. "Lucy was a vixen in the bedroom. I always wondered where she learned how to be such a good cock tease."

Rebecca's patience with him was gone and he knew it. Marco offensively wrapped his hand around her neck before she could retaliate. Smiling down at her, he squeezed. She kept his steady gaze and endured the assault, refusing to give into his arrogance.

"The car's ready." He let go of her neck.

She took a small breath and left the drama behind. She brushed her hair back and glared at him.

"Time to go, princess." He snapped handcuffs around her wrists. "Get the briefcase and put her in the truck."

He threaded his hands in her hair, her mother's necklace dropped onto her chest. It rested just beneath her collar. Before she could react, a rough hand grabbed her arm, pulling her out of the room.

Led to the back of the house, the thug opened the glass door before he pushed her through. She saw the familiar black SUV waiting. She scanned the area and realized there were only two thugs in the immediate area. She walked with him until the sun hit her face and she took her opportunity.

Rebecca doubled over and screamed in false pain. Her thug crouched down to reclaim her arm. She linked her hands and hit him on the back of the neck. He fell forward and she smashed her knee into his face.

She ran. An unexpected second thug appeared from behind the SUV. Two seconds too late, her attempt to maneuver around him failed as her right ankle rolled to the side.

She ran into him with maximum force and took him down with her as she fell. She landed on her shoulder and pushed herself up. Her legs beneath her, she rose when a boot crashed into her ribs. Thrown back onto the ground, she gasped for air.

The faint echo of sirens pushed off the desert wind. Yanked to her feet, she used every ounce of her energy to get away. Her knee thrust into her current captor's groin. He fell away, but a second thug grabbed her by the waist. She jabbed at him with her elbows. He lifted her off the ground and dragged her toward the truck. The sirens got closer and she screamed. Marco barked orders. A hand covered her mouth. She continued to fight.

"Get her in the truck!"

CHAPTER TWO

Eric turned onto a sand-covered road with a large house in the distance. Charlie handed him his vest as he took the wheel so Eric could pull it over his shoulders.

"There are extra clips in the box under the seat."

The house was extravagant. Big difference from the shack they apparently inhabited hours before.

Eric stopped the truck about fifty feet from the front and got out. He adjusted his vest as he waited for Charlie to join him. The Boulder Sheriff's team pulled in beside them. Signaling to the sheriffs to take the back, he and Charlie headed for the front.

They crossed the rock-covered yard, but before they could step up to the estate, two gunshots rang out. They both ducked for cover. They searched for the shooter. Eric found Charlie, who had a better angle on the porch. Charlie signaled and he nodded. He walked the opposite direction. The distraction got the shooter's attention. Two more shots fired and Eric hit the ground. The sound of pounding footsteps followed by a crash came from the front of the house.

"Charlie!"

"God damn it!" Eric jogged up the steps into the house. He stepped through the door, gun raised and turned the corner, seeing Charlie.

"He took off out the window."

"Tell BCS, they'll catch him."

Charlie nodded before disappearing.

The Boulder County Sheriff's department secured the area. Eric moved through the house, going room by room, looking for any trace of her. He pushed open a door and stopped. Oddly enough, he could smell her. The faint scent of peach hit him and he ventured further into the room. Seeing nothing of consequence, he moved to the bathroom, pushing open the door.

He immediately saw makeup on the counter and a brush. His eyes wandered while his heart pounded. He found jeans, a t-shirt and sneakers in the corner. He picked up the t-shirt, immediately hit with her scent. He turned to see a discarded lace black dress. He picked up the dress, noticing that it was dirty and ripped. He looked at the tub and found a towel hanging over the side. Touching it, he found it was still damp. The towel shifted and slipped onto the floor. He turned, seeing the drop of red. He lifted the towel and saw a stain of blood, his breath halting in his lungs.

He shook off the paralyzing fear that clutched him. He took the dress with him as he moved out of the bedroom. There was a line of officers gathered at the far end of the hall and Eric followed them to a doorway. He stopped, seeing another basement.

"Charlie?" Eric followed the sound of voices down the stairs. When he reached the bottom, his eyes refocused to see Charlie in the corner looking at a small area. "What did you find?"

"Eric, hey, it's nothing," Charlie crossed the room to meet him. "We should . . ."

Eric ignored him and stepped forward. He took in what everyone was focused on. A small area on the right side of the basement, in the corner. Ordinary enough until you realized what you were looking at was a prison. The thick chain started at the wall of pipes and ended at the two-inch-thick iron manacles waiting on the floor. The sight hit him and he stopped breathing.

"Detective Stiles," someone called and Charlie moved him toward the stairs.

Eric regained some of his senses but teetered on the edge of destruction as they stepped out into the sunshine.

"We picked him up a few miles down the road. Says Valnes left just before we got here."

"Where did he go?" Eric stepped toward the man.

"I would suggest you tell him. He's really not in a good mood," Charlie added when the man didn't respond.

"Where is he?"

"Valnes has a meeting."

"Was there a woman with him?"

The man once again hesitated.

"Talk!"

"He took the girl with him. I think she's a part of the deal."

"Where?"

"I . . . I don't know. The buyer set it up, not him. He never told us where they were going."

"How long ago did they leave?"

"Right before you got here. They heard the sirens and took off down the back road."

Charlie and Eric left the man to the locals and bounded to the truck, speeding off in the direction of the back road.

"Okay, what's around here?" Eric scanned the horizon.

"Not much."

"Where are we thinking this road is going to lead?" Charlie looked at the GPS.

"The airport."

"What?"

"If we keep going this direction, we're headed straight to the Boulder City Municipal Airport."

Marco opened the truck door and pulled her out beside him. Grabbing her wrist, Marco dragged her forward. He walked toward a large, closed hangar and she followed. The orange of the setting sun reflected off the wavy metal walls. They reached the door and Marco opened it for her as she stepped inside.

Open space. The first thing that caught Rebecca's eye was the pearl white jet stream shadowed against the wall. Behind it, the edge of a window looked into a large office. Covered pallets and rows of individual tool stations lined the walls. A silver Mercedes parked beside her, right next to a black SUV.

That's original . . . what, is there a bad guy manual with a list of minimum requirements? Black SUV, gold chains, hairy chest, bad breath, obnoxious fashion sense.

They continued to walk when a stone-faced thug man met them. Her stomach clenched in recognition, her skin crawling at the memory of his hands on her body.

You're mine . . .

The two groups met in the middle of the large space. Marco stopped and she halted beneath his gripping hands. She searched for something, anything to help her get out of there.

"Now that we're all here, let's not waste any time," the unnamed man said, his accent thick and heady like his hands. "I have a schedule to keep."

"Agreed," Marco arrogantly puffed out his chest.

The accented man waved to an unknown person. A moment later, a man appeared with a silver briefcase in his hand. Rebecca watched Marco's motion as well. Marco released her arm and moved forward, a silver briefcase in his hand, too. Her curiosity piqued. She wondered what exactly was about to happen.

A thug took the silver briefcase from Marco and placed it on a nearby chair before he proceeded to open it. Foam padding surrounded a small black box and the accented man moved to examine it. He lifted it out of the case, looked it over and turned to Marco in question.

"Not until I have my money," Marco demanded in a low tone.

Rebecca watched as the man looked to Marco and then waved his man forward with the second briefcase. He rested the case in his arms and opened it, revealing more money than she could ever fathom. Her eyes went to the accented man and found him staring at her, his gaze roaming her body. She averted her eyes.

"Where is it?"

Rebecca felt Marco move. His hands were in her hair and then rested on her shoulders before they slid down her chest, framing the necklace.

"Come here," the accented man requested. A wanton smile spread across his lips and she felt Marco un-cuffing her hands.

"Walk," Marco commanded into her ear. She shifted uncomfortably before taking a few steps toward the accented man.

"Delicious."

"Stop," he commanded.

She turned and faced Marco, his gun raised and aimed at her chest.

"I'm listening," the accented man said.

"You'll take my men and me to New York. It's on your way. Shouldn't be too much of a problem, right?" As if on cue, the main hangar door opened to reveal a half a dozen of Marco's goons. Guns raised.

"Fine." Footsteps came up behind her before an arm snaked around her waist. "But the girl is mine to take, free of charge."

Rebecca waited, doing her best to hide the waves of revulsion as he pulled her tight against him. Marco lowered his weapon with a wide smile. He motioned to his men and they lowered their weapons.

Rebecca released a hesitant breath.

Crisis averted.

"Now that we have an understanding, why don't you join me for a drink?" His hand spread over her abdomen.

Marco nodded in agreement and mumbled something to the thug to his right. The man nodded and looked at his counterpart before taking position on either side of the main door. The arm around her waist slid to her back. He ushered her across the hangar. They reached the office and the accented man opened the door.

The room was much more luxurious than she would have guessed. Plush cream carpeting beneath her feet and the walls were a pale green. It was furnished with two cream-colored couches and several matching chairs. Lush green plants framed a warm oak desk and chair on the opposite wall. The door closed behind her and Marco sat down in one of the chairs. The accented man moved toward the inset wet bar behind the door.

"Please, have a seat, my dear," he began to pour their drinks.

"Do you have a ladies room I could use?"

"Of course," he motioned toward the back of the room.

She saw a shadowed area in the back corner. She moved toward it and turned the corner. Face to face with two armed men, she stifled a gasp of surprise. She stilled until they let her pass.

She eyed the door to the bathroom, turned the knob and stepped inside. The tiny personal bathroom offered nothing as far as assistance in her plight. She used the facility and washed her hands before passing her reflection in irritation.

She stepped into the hallway, met once again by the two

men. She smiled at them, but they didn't move out of her way. Rebecca attempted to go around them. They stopped her. She was about to object when she heard a loud bang. She jumped back and looked to the men in confusion, her heart pounding in her chest.

They stepped out of her way. She timidly walked into the main office. It took a moment before she absorbed the spatter of blood and brains on the wall. Marco was seated but not moving. The blood drained from her face as she struggled for air.

"I apologize for the vulgar display. Mr. Valnes' demands were quite unreasonable," the accented man explained plainly as he approached. "He was a vile, detestable piece of scum. The world will be a better place without him."

Her head swam in shock, confusion and revulsion. An arm encircled her waist from behind. He pulled her against him and her stomach lurched. His hand brushed her hair away from her neck. She couldn't stop the tremble that shook her spine. She felt his breath and then lips on her neck.

"Hanger G34," Eric turned the SUV into the Boulder City Municipal Airport. "It's the only hanger with a filed flight plan for this evening.

"Did you call the tower? I want everything grounded. Nothing leaves until we find her!"

"Got it."

"How far behind is the cavalry?"

"Two minutes."

"Tell them to make it one, or we're going in without them."

"Stiles."

"I can't wait, Lug."

"Watch your back."

"That's what Charlie's here for. See you on the other side," Eric ended the call. "Do you see it?"

"Should be coming up around the next corner."

Eric slowed as five black SUVs came into view. "I see ten, maybe twelve men."

"Yeah, and they're all together," pointing out that the majority of the armed men were gathered in the far corner of the hangar.

"What do you have in mind?"

Chapter Three

Her body revolted against the affection. She tried to pull away from him. He held her firm, but the feel of her skin crawling was too powerful. She continued to struggle against him. His free hand began groping her body. She couldn't suppress the tears of anger that began to fall down her cheeks.

He spun her around. His hand wrapped around her neck. He forced her to face him.

"The harder you fight, the more I know you enjoy it," his thumb traced her lip. "Your fire is fueling and beautiful . . ."

The room shook with the power of an explosion. He looked away from her in hesitation before grabbing her wrist. He said something in German. The two men hidden in the back of the office appeared and ran out of the room.

Rebecca strained to look out the window, curious about what was happening. An explosion against her cheek sent her falling back. He yanked her back, a gleam of triumph in his eyes. Her fury piqued. She spat in his face. Her stiletto became a dagger and she shoved it into the top of his foot.

It stuck and he bellowed in anger. She pried herself out of his hands and discarded the entrenched shoe. She grabbed one of the whiskey bottles off the bar. He lurched toward her and she smashed it on the back of his head.

The black SUV to the right of the center of activity exploded. Eric watched the team of armed men scramble toward it before he blew the lock off the door. Eric kicked it in and Charlie followed. The ruse led the armed entourage into the waiting arms of the Narcotics team. All they needed to do now was find Rebecca and get out.

Eric took in the large space. Seeing an office on the opposite wall, he decided to start there. Two men opened fire. Eric rolled behind a black SUV while Charlie took cover behind a large pallet. Eric peered over the hood of the truck in an attempt to identify their shooters when two more appeared.

He took two shots. One hit a shoulder, knocking its victim back. The other hit the plane behind him. Eric ducked back as the gunfire focused on him.

He moved to the opposite end of the truck. He needed to get past these idiots. He looked to Charlie. His brother read his mind. On the count of three, Charlie laid down cover fire. Eric crossed the corner of the room. He made his way along the wall toward the office. A man appeared from behind the plane with his gun pointed at Eric's chest. The thundering of metal echoed off the tin walls and his attacker looked away. Eric embraced the distraction and took a shot. He hit the man in the leg and he fell back. Eric knocked the gun out of his hand.

Eric spun to resume his journey. His jaw exploded. His head smacked the ground with a thud and his gun slid out of his hand.

An oversized human refrigerator stampeded toward him. Eric scrambled to his feet. A pair of hands landed on his shoulders. They pulled him back. He used the momentum to step back. He reached around and gripped his assailant by the arm. Eric dropped his shoulder and pulled him forward. With a swift motion, he tossed him on the ground. The thug was stunned.

Eric made his escape and reached the office. A large crash,

followed by shouting erupted to his right. Eric turned toward the noise and saw a flash of red.

Rebecca . . .

She stayed low and moved along the wall.

Her progress steady, she managed to remain unnoticed. A twinge rose in her side and she ignored it. After several more steps, the twinge became a slicing pain. It dug into her body and forced her to stop. She tried to breathe it away, but it only intensified. Her hand immediately went to her abdomen in agony. The surge was slowly splitting her in half.

Biting back the pain, she pushed herself to move, her focus on the opening at the end of the hangar. She shifted forward when an arm curled around her neck with a growl. She instinctively thrust an elbow into his ribs. The blow was weak and she cursed her body as his grip tightened.

"Let's go," his accent sent a chill up her spine.

He pushed her along the wall toward the same destination. He kept them low in an attempt not to draw any attention.

Rebecca regained some of her strength. She fought back. Whoever was shooting in the hangar was obviously no friend of his. If she could get their attention on him, she could slip away. She did her best to get away. He was stronger and his grip on her tightening with each attempt.

Rebecca searched for a way out, something to help when the twinge in her side began to erupt again.

No, not now!

She saw a tool rack a few feet away. She quickened to pull him off balance. This gave her enough room to kick outward and knock it over. It caused a reverberating crash that was quickly lost in the swell of gunfire.

He grabbed her arm with a menacing glare. His urgency

to escape was clearly defined in his threatening eyes.

Twenty feet from the door, they would be clear of the edge of the warehouse within moments. He thrust her into the night air. His hand remained firmly clenched around her arm, pulling her along. The twinge in her side strengthened and she slowed in response, gasping for air.

He shoved the gun into her ribs to propel her forward. She saw the waiting car in the distance and she'd had enough. Panic and self-preservation overrode any fear. She resisted and forced him to stop. He turned, lowering the butt of his gun against her shoulder. She collapsed to her knees in a yelp of pain. He yanked her back to her feet by her hair. She stood and continued to twist her arm in an attempt to break free, despite the pain.

"Stop."

The accented man dug the gun into her ribs as he yanked her in front of him.

Eric stumbled into the night air. He heard her cry out in pain. She was on the ground and the man yanked her to her feet by her hair. He saw her and his heart raced faster, running to catch them.

"Stop!"

His gun raised, Eric watched the man turn and pull her in front of him. She continued to fight, despite the gun in her ribs.

"Let her go." His body and mind calmed with the tension.

The man sneered.

Eric watched Rebecca react to the sound of his voice, her expression showing shocked disbelief. He met her eyes. His heart screamed for her as he watched her take a breath.

She's okay.

"This is none of your concern. Go back to your little raid and leave us be, or I'll be forced to kill her."

Eric restrained his biting fury." You're going to let her go and I'm going to not kill you." His voice was strong and aggressive against the threat.

Just let her go.

Just let her go.

"Who do you think you're dealing with, officer?"

"Scum."

The European man's grip tightened around her arm.

Eric needed her to move so he could get a shot off and end this. He looked to Rebecca in an attempt to communicate. His heart stopped as she doubled over in agony. Her body curled into its self as she dropped to the ground.

He pulled the trigger twice.

"Rebecca!"

The man took injuries in the leg and shoulder. Eric watched him fall back. Rebecca lifted herself off the ground. Eric moved without thought. She screamed his name. A blistering fire knocked him off his feet.

"Eric!" she screamed in horror. "No!"

Rebecca pushed her body across the space between them and dropped to her knees. She rolled him onto his back and undid the straps to his vest. She lifted it to reveal a growing stain of blood on his shirt.

"Beccs."

She crouched over him, her hands cupping his face as she met his eyes. "I'm here," her eyes filled with tears.

"Hey, beautiful," he touched the curls framing her face.

"Hey, hero," she gripped his hand and he tried to move.

"We've got to get you out of here." He moved to sit up and his face tightened in agony.

"Baby, lay still," she gently pushed him back. "I have to try and stop the bleeding until help gets here." She caressed his face and he lay back. She covered the wound with her hands. She applied pressure to stop the bleeding and heard him growl in pain. His blood continued to spill around her hands and she began to panic, tears streaming down her cheeks. She looked at him when his eyes began to close.

"No, Eric, look at me," she kept her hand in place but leaned forward, calling to him. "Stay with me, baby. Please, Eric, look at me!"

"I love you, Beccs," he touched her cheek in a tender caress.

No, no, please, God, please don't take him . . .

"Eric," she started as his hand fell limp and her heart stopped. "No, Eric . . . no . . . please stay with me . . ."

Eric please . . . I can't do this without you . . . please . . .

Her entire body sobbed in panic.

His chest continued to rise and fall. He wasn't done yet.

Rebecca pushed her tears away, corralled her emotions and focused on his wound. She kept the pressure constant while she tried to think of what to do.

"Get up!"

Her eyes rose to see one of Marco's thugs. His gun was aimed at her and she realized it was the man who'd shot Eric. "No."

"Get up!"

"Leave me alone!"

"Get up, whore!"

"If you're going to kill me, then do it. I'm not moving!"

He studied her and then grabbed her arm to pull her away.

"No, let go." She saw Eric's gun.

He pulled her away, but she fought hard. He lost his grip. She broke free from his grasp. She lunged for the gun as he caught her hair. She gripped the weapon, spun and fired. The bullet hit square in the chest and he looked at her in disbelief. Rebecca fell back in shock as the thug hit the ground. The world paused for a moment.

She told her body to take a breath and then it complied. The world started again.

Rebecca laid the weapon on the ground and turned to Eric. Her hands and focus returned to Eric's wound.

She heard footsteps and acknowledged the gun beside her knee. As they got closer, she trembled and reached for the weapon. She stayed beside Eric, her hand continuing to press against his wound. She stared into the darkness, waiting for her next opponent to appear. Her body tightened, constricting her lungs in terror.

Charlie moved into the light.

"Charlie!"

Her body sobbed in relief. Within moments, she felt him next to her and looked to him as he stared in shock at Eric. "Help me!"

He snapped out of his trance and turned to call for help.

She felt him taking the gun out of her hand and as soon as it disappeared, she pressed on Eric's wound with both hands.

"Beccs."

"I can't . . . I can't stop the bleeding! My hands aren't enough. I need something to cover the wound." She searched for something, anything to help. The blood continued to spill over her hands.

Charlie pulled off his shirt. He handed it to her.

Folding it in half, she laid it on Eric's stomach. She leaned forward, lifted her legs and reapplied pressure to the wound.

"Beccs . . . let me . . ."

"Put your hands on top of mine and push," she replied breathless. Her heart thudded in her ears as he followed her directions. "Where's the ambulance?"

"They're coming."

"We have to stop the bleeding," she said as the shirt

soaked up the blood.

All of her energy focused on keeping him alive. She never heard the sirens when the ambulance arrived. Men in blue shirts surrounded her and someone lifted her off the ground. She couldn't move. She couldn't breathe as she watched the medical team treat him. A gentle hand rested in her hair. It guided her cheek to a warm shoulder.

They lifted him onto a stretcher and she moved to his side. Rebecca grasped Eric's hand as she sat down in the ambulance. A blanket wrapped around her and she turned in exhaustion. Charlie appeared and took the seat beside her in the ambulance, his reassuring hand resting on her back.

In an instant, her shock melted into raw terror. Her body shook uncontrolled. Her forehead propped in her hand. She attempted to regain control. Her chest denied her request. Instead, heaving sobs of helplessness from her lips. Charlie's arms wrapped around her shoulders.

Eric remained stable throughout the trip to the hospital. Rebecca followed them inside, Charlie at her side.

"You'll have to wait here," a nurse said as they wheeled him away from her.

"What? No, I have to . . ." Charlie's hands gently gripped her arms.

"We'll come update you as soon as we can."

"Wait, no . . . please."

The nurse disappeared behind the door.

"Beccs," she turned into him.

"Charlie, I can't . . . I have to stay with him."

"Let the doctors do what they need to do. They'll come and get us as soon as they can."

"No, I can't . . ."

"Rebecca, you need to calm down."

"I'm not going to calm down . . . he's been shot, Charlie!"

"Beccs . . ."

"He's bleeding . . . he needs me. I have to find a way . . ."

"You have to get checked out by a doctor."

"I'm fine."

"No you're not."

"I'm not leaving him!"

"Rebecca, you need to listen to me."

"No, Charlie, I'm fine! I don't need a doctor—"

"Beccs, look at me," he turned her around.

She was forced to face him.

"I'm taking you to see a doctor."

"Charlie . . ."

"Beccs," he hesitated. "You're pregnant."

She heard the words, but they seemed foreign somehow. Garbled in her ears and she shook her head in confusion.

"Yes, sweetheart."

The nausea, the dizzy spells.

The pain.

Pregnant.

"Oh God . . ." Her knees weakened in panic. "Charlie . . ."

Her breath escaped her when she tried to tell him. Then his face disappeared behind the gray. She was lifted into the air. Her heart sobbed as she fell into blackness.

The fog over her eyes began to lift and she felt a warm hand around hers. Rebecca opened her eyes, expecting to see Eric. She saw Charlie instead and the panic of events came flooding back.

"Charlie . . ." Her eyes immediately filled with tears.

"Just relax, the doctor is on the way," he gently squeezed her hand.

Despite his warmth, her fear took hold and she struggled against her own lungs. The room began to swim and the twinge returned. "Charlie!" Her hand went to her abdomen.

"Rebecca, breathe. You need to breathe."

"Something's wrong." The staggering pain hit and she cried out. "Charlie . . ."

His hand disappeared.

She heard people entering the room. The pain intensified and she cried out again, hearing muffled voices. She opened her eyes.

Charlie stared back, his eyes revealing his own fear. He held onto her hand and she cried, silently pleading for relief.

The baby . . . please, no.

The pain slowly began to subside, but she continued to cry, unable to let go of her fear.

"Rebecca."

She faced him and he moved closer, his hand smoothing the hair on her forehead.

"You have to stop crying. You need to calm down, sweetheart."

"Rebecca, you need to relax. You're making it worse," a nurse said, sitting on the bed next to her. "We've given you some medication to help, but you need to calm down and let it work."

Rebecca tried to take a breath. It shuddered as it hit her lungs. She could feel herself tensing again, the entire world overwhelming her.

"Beccs, listen to me."

Tears streamed down her face.

"I know that you're tired, worried and scared, but you have to be strong now. The baby needs you to be the fiery, stubborn, brilliant woman I know. I'm going to be right here with you, so just hang on to me. You can do this."

His gaze was reassuring and kind as it fell on her. She forced the tears and paralyzing fear away as she took a deep breath.

"That's it," he said with a smile, her head resting into the pillow. "Deep breaths, nice and easy. You realize you're not just breathing for you and my niece or nephew. You're breathing for me because if I screw this up, my brother is going to kill me."

"Eric knows about the baby?" Her heart started to calm.

"He's the one who told me." Charlie gave her a soothing smile. "Dr. Raines called when he found out you were missing. He thought Eric needed to know."

She thought about him, bleeding, struggling and her body flooded with worry. She could feel herself beginning to crumble again. The beeping of monitors screamed. She tried to gulp it back, but couldn't stop the tears that began to fall.

"Beccs." His thumb brushed the crown of her head. "He's going to be okay. He wouldn't want you to worry. He practically killed himself to find you. A bullet isn't going to stop him."

Rebecca inhaled a deep breath and nodded. She knew everything he said was true but continued to struggle with the billowing fear.

"He would want you focused on you and the baby."

She began to relax again.

"He loves you and would never leave you. You need to trust him."

Eric's frustrated face appeared in her mind and she took another breath. She imagined his arms wrapped around her, telling her it was going to be okay. She could do this. Slowly, the monitors stopped beeping and she felt herself sinking into the pillow beneath her.

The door opened again and a smiling woman in a lab coat entered the room. "Rebecca?"

"Yes, I'm Rebecca."

"Hi, I am Dr. Hagadorn. How are you feeling?" She moved around the bed and two of the nurses exited the room.

"I'm not sure."

"You are the father?" She held out her hand to Charlie.

"Uncle. Charlie," he shook the doctor's hand.

"It looks like we are reducing the stress on the fetus and slowly getting your blood pressure down." She looked over her chart. "You've been having some abdominal pain?"

"Yes."

"Have you noticed any spotting?"

"No."

"Okay, let's take a look." The doctor reached for a large white machine on wheels. The remaining nurses exited the room, leaving her and Charlie alone with the doctor.

Rebecca watched her turn on the machine.

She pulled on Rebecca's gown, revealing her abdomen. "This is going to be a little cold."

It was only then that Rebecca realized her dress was missing and replaced with a hospital gown. The doctor squirted some cool jelly on her skin before placing a handheld monitor over her stomach. She turned toward the monitor and followed the doctor's eyes. She began to see something. It was a fuzzy blurb until she stopped. It came into focus. A large black blurb with a little gray mass off to one side.

"There's your baby," the doctor continued to look at the monitor, moving the mouse as she took measurements.

"Is it okay?"

"Looks good."

Rebecca felt Charlie squeeze her hand. "How pregnant am I?"

"I'd guess a little over six weeks," she said as she hit a button on the machine.

Rebecca heard a whirling sound before the doctor pulled turned off the monitor and handed her a tissue. "So the baby's okay?"

"For now." She turned back to them with kind eyes. "But the stress you and your baby have been through has put both of you at risk. We are going to need to monitor both of you for a few days to see how things progress. Which means staying in bed, resting and no stress. Physical or emotional."

The doctor looked to Rebecca and Charlie.

"I understand that there are extenuating circumstances, so just do your best. If there's any more pain or if you start spotting, I want you to call the nurse immediately. Try and sleep, your body needs to recover from the trauma and settle back into itself. We'll know more in the morning, okay?"

Rebecca nodded, fear welling in her throat. She looked to Charlie, who smiled in reassurance. She took a deep breath.

The doctor rose from her seat on the bed. She turned, handing her two pieces of paper. "Here are my instructions. This," she said with a smile, "is your first baby picture."

Rebecca looked down at it, still in disbelief. "Thank you so much."

"Take care, Rebecca. It was nice to meet you, Charlie."

"You, too, thanks so much for everything."

She nodded and moved through the door to leave.

The door closed and Rebecca leaned back into the pillow.

"Are you okay?" Charlie looked at her, concerned.

"Yeah, just . . . processing, I guess," she said, the picture of her baby in her hand. She was unable not to stare at it.

They heard a knock and Charlie rose to open the door. "Beccs, you have a visitor," he pushed open the door, revealing Lucy.

Lucy walked to the bed.

Rebecca smiled, enveloping her in a hug. "Hey, sweetie."

"Beccs." Lucy pulled back, tears in her eyes. "I'm so glad you're okay. I'm so sorry."

"What for?"

"This is all my fault and then I left you there alone

and . . ."

"No, sweetie, no. None of this is your fault, don't even think that." Rebecca wiped away her sister's tears. "It's over and we're okay."

"The nurse said that Eric was shot and he's—"

"Going to be fine," Charlie quickly cut in.

Rebecca took a breath, trying not to overreact. "So he's in surgery now?"

"He went in about half an hour ago."

He reached out to squeeze Rebecca's hand as she reminded herself to breathe.

"They said barring any complications, the surgery should take about three hours."

"What's this," Lucy asked, seeing the black and white photo on her lap.

"That is the first picture of your niece or nephew." She was a little hesitant about her sister's reaction to the news.

"Are you serious?"

"Very."

"Oh my God, Beccs!" Lucy looked at the picture with a huge smile. "That's amazing. I'm so happy for you!"

"Thanks, Lucy." Her sister gave her another hug. Rebecca saw Charlie pick up the list of instructions the doctor left for her. His phone buzzed and he looked down at it.

"Dad is on the way and you need to eat. So I'm going to meet Dad, get us all something to eat and then I'll be back." He looked at her in silent hesitation.

"Sounds like a plan."

Lucy rose from her seat on Rebecca's bed. "I'll be right back," Lucy said, following Charlie out of the room.

Lying back, her mind drifted to Eric. She hoped that he knew just how much she loved him. The call of exhaustion was too strong and her eyes became unbearably heavy. Her aching body relaxed into the cushion of the bed. Her eyes slipped close and she drifted off.

Rebecca shifted and her eyes slowly opened. She looked around to see Lucy, reading a magazine.

"Beccs, you're awake," she put the magazine aside, walking to her bed. "How are you feeling?"

"Good. How long have I been asleep?"

"A couple of hours maybe."

"Is Eric out of surgery yet?"

"I'm not sure, Charlie went to find out. I met Charlie and Eric's dad, he's really nice."

"Harry is a wonderful man," she said, leaning back into the pillow, her head throbbing.

"So I was thinking, with everything that's happened, Eric recovering from surgery and you and the baby being on bed rest, what would you think about me moving in for a little while to help out?"

"I, uh, I love that you're offering and of course, I would love it if you stayed with us, but you need to focus on your own recovery, sweetie."

"Beccs, I can handle it," Lucy insisted, becoming defensive. "I'm better, really."

"Lucy, it's not a matter of whether or not you can handle it. I'm sure that you can."

"Then what is it?"

"I just think you need to finish your therapy before we start talking about—"

"God, I'm such an idiot." Lucy rose from the bed, crossing her arms over her chest in frustration.

"No you're not."

"I can't believe I let you convince me that you actually cared about me!"

"What are you talking about? Of course I care about you!"

"No, you don't! I don't fit into your perfect little life and you want me to just disappear."

"Lucy, you know that's not true." Rebecca reminded herself to stay calm. "You're my sister, I want you in my life, I always will."

"Oh please, you have Eric, Charlie, Donna and Harry. They're your family now. There's no room for me anymore. I've been replaced."

"Lucy, stop, you know that's not—" Her heart raced and her chest tightened.

No stress . . .

"Yes, it is. You're just too much of a coward to admit it, Beccs. You've always been a coward."

"Honey, I love you, but I can't do this with you right now."

"Of course you can't." The bitterness evident in her eyes, Lucy moved across the room to the door. "That's okay. I'm used to being put on the back burner. The damn baby gets more sympathy than I do and it's not even born yet!"

"Lucy . . ." Her heart broke as the door closed and Rebecca let her sister go. Helpless as to what to do, she took a deep breath.

She fought to breathe through the anxiety, telling herself not to get upset. She hated being so emotional and despite her efforts, the tears began to fall. It felt completely stupid, but she desperately wanted Eric. Knowing that she couldn't see him made it that much worse.

Her tears came hard and fast while she repeatedly told herself to calm down. A twinge in her side got her attention. She suppressed the panic it brought. Her hand brushed through her hair in resilience, wiping the relentless tears from her eyes. There was a knock on the door and she heard Charlie's voice.

"Hey, hey, what's wrong?" He saw her tears and sat down.

"Nothing . . . hormones." Her voice cracked in emotion

and he gently took her hand. "How is he?"

"He's out of surgery and he's stable. There's nothing to be worried about."

"How bad was it?"

"They're saying he'll make a full recovery."

She released a breath she didn't realize she was holding and then saw the hesitation in his eyes. "What are you not telling me?"

"It's doesn't matter now, he is fine." He tried to soothe her.

She immediately felt patronized by the effort. "No, if he were fine, you wouldn't be scared to tell me what happened." Her eyes watered in anger and fear.

"Beccs, breathe."

"Just tell me what's going on."

"When they got him into surgery, they found that the bullet did more damage than they'd initially thought." He watched her carefully, the worry apparent in his eyes. "I guess at one point, his blood pressure bottomed out and his heart stopped."

"Charlie . . ."

"But he's okay. They restarted his heart and the rest of the surgery went fine."

"Where is he now?" Rebecca wiped the wetness away from her eyes, fighting the rising panic in her chest.

"In recovery."

"What happens now?"

"We wait and see what happens when he wakes up." He squeezed her hand in reassurance.

She silently nodded, unable to articulate anything beyond the breath of Eric's name. Charlie leaned forward and wrapped her in a warm hug. She reached around his chest and clung to him in terror, her hands digging into his back.

"He's going to be okay," he whispered into her hair as he

rubbed her back.

"I can't lose him, Charlie," her voice wavering when she tried not to cry.

"You're not going to, I promise." Charlie pulled back, looking into her eyes. "I promise you, he's going to be fine, okay?"

She nodded and took a deep breath, blinking back the curling emotion in her chest.

"It's late, get some sleep."

Her body sunk into the pillow and he pulled the blankets over her legs.

"I'll be back in the morning to check on you."

Charlie turned off the main light and flashed her a smile before disappearing behind the door.

The pooling in her gut overflowed and Rebecca tugged the thin blanket up to her chin. She tried desperately to breathe through it, but the tears came anyway. They fell slow and steady and she curled into fetal position.

Her mind wouldn't stop.

She couldn't close her eyes.

She lay focused on the window in the corner of the room. It was tiny, only revealing a few soft, faint beams as they danced on the floor. Rebecca wasn't sure how long she'd been laying in the dark when the door opened. She shifted, seeing the nurse walk into the room. The nurse checked her IV before looking down at her in concern.

"What are you still doing awake?" She turned on the small overhead light.

"What time is it?"

"After four. Do you want something to help you sleep?"

"No, I don't think I should . . ."

"Don't worry about that. I can give you something mild that won't affect the baby."

Rebecca's eyes began to tear and she pushed out a sigh of

frustration.

"What's going on that's got you so upset?"

"No, Eric, look at me," she pleaded, her warm hands on his cheek. "Stay with me baby, stay with me."

"I love you, Beccs." He touched her cheek. The softness beneath his thumb was soothing as his energy began to fade.

"Eric," he heard her call when he fell away into the darkness. "No, please stay with me . . ."

"Rebecca." Eric struggled to open his eyes.

He tried to focus, his eyes still heavy in exhaustion. He recalled waking in the hospital earlier, seeing a nurse staring back at him. He was exhausted, so he slipped back into slumber. Now he opened his eyes again, his body wasn't as heavy. He had the need to stretch and he shifted, twisting his back. There was throbbing pain and biting it back, he relaxed. His eyes adjusted to the room. Random pieces of his life floated in his mind. His conscious awoke and he remembered the dream.

But it wasn't a dream.

Rebecca.

His heart pounded and he commanded his body to move. He noticed a heavy warmth against his chest. Eric looked down and his heart soared in relief. She was asleep against his chest. His arm wrapped around her as he blinked back the wetness in his eyes. The softness of her hair beneath his fingers verified she was real. He took a deep breath and his heart calmed.

He shifted to pull her closer. His side protested. He ignored it and continued to move. He was able to face her while she slept in the curve of his shoulder.

Eric found himself in quiet awe of her beauty and how much he loved her. The soft curls of her hair twisted within his fingers and he reveled in the fact that he could touch her at all. The bruises that covered her and the IV in her hand, stabbed at him and he let out a slow anguish-filled breath.

He leaned forward and kissed her forehead, his thumb lining her bruised cheek. With an unimaginable ache to pull her closer, his touch pulled her out of her slumber and her eyes fluttered open.

"Hey, bright eyes."

"Eric." Her eyes widened before she threw her arms around his neck. He pulled her against him and closed his eyes as a second wave of relief washed over him.

"Oh God." She strained to pull away, her voice still just above a whisper. "Am I hurting you? I should go get the doctor."

"No, not yet." He kept his arms locked around her and she met his eyes. Seeing worry, fear and apprehension, he brushed her cheek with the back of his hand. "It can wait, you can't."

"Are you in pain?"

"Yes," his fingers caressed the edge of her hair before tucking it behind her ear. "But we aren't talking about me right now. I want to talk about you."

"You're the one who got shot, hero." She leaned against him and lined his jaw with her fingertip.

"Beccs . . ." he felt her body tense and his heart ached. He couldn't help but hear her screams from the phone recording.

She looked away, a deep shuddering breath escaped her lips and she sunk into his shoulder. "I didn't know. How could I not have not known . . ." She scolded herself between pain-filled gasps. "Everything that happened, I could've . . . we almost . . ."

"Stop, baby." She trembled in his arms. He watched as her mind took her to all the horrid places he didn't know about yet.

"I'm so scared."

He saw her eyes brimming with tears. He placed a tender hand over her stomach. His heart raced in absolute love and unwavering devotion. Eric took a deep breath, savoring the feel of their child beneath his hand. "Our baby, this little person, is strong and so is its mother."

Her hands rested over his with a smile. His entire world swept perfectly into a magnetic shade of blue as she captured his eyes.

"I love you so much." Tears edging her eyes, she traced the line of his jaw with her finger. She searched his eyes before her soft lips melted against his and he drowned in their sweetness. His heart gasped again at the thought of almost losing her when she broke the embrace. Her eyes locked with his, she caressed his face. His heart finally calmed and she smiled.

"I love you, too."

"You're going to be a wonderful father," she twisted away from him and then turned back to him with something in her hand.

"What's this?"

"Our first baby picture."

A shining smile lit her face and his hand lifted off her stomach to take the photo. Eric stared at the black and gray blob in his hand. He wondered if they needed more light and feeling like a bumbling fool, he looked back to her in confusion. "What exactly am I looking at?" Her giggle made him smile.

She leaned into his shoulder and pointed to the gray blob at the bottom of the photo. "That's our baby."

"And what's the black?"

"My uterus," she said with patient understanding.

"Ah, that makes sense," he touched the photo in fascination. "So you're both okay?"

"Yes."

Eric moved, unable to suppress a groan of pain.

She looked to him in concern. "I'm going to get the doctor."

"I'm fine," he insisted, pulling her closer. "What did the doctor say?"

"Eric . . ."

"What did the doctor say?"

"She said so far everything looks okay." She curled into him.

He could feel her body beginning to tense.

"But she also said that at this stage of the pregnancy, we're going to have to be careful. Especially after everything that's already happened."

"You told her what happened at the airport?"

"Yes," she looked up at him as he stroked her hair. "She said that the stress I've been . . . we've been under is affecting . . ."

Hearing her stop, his hand gently tangled itself within the folds of her hair.

"The stress is affecting the baby." She met his eyes with apprehension as he continued to play with her hair. "They are going to keep me here for a few days to monitor the baby and make sure everything is okay. She said I need rest and absolutely no stress."

"Then that's what's going to happen," his thumb stroked her temple.

She moved into his chest. "Eric, you just got out of surgery," she tensed again within his arms. "We haven't even spoken to the police about what happened or Marco. All of this is far from over. How are we going to —"

"You let me worry about that." He kissed the top of her head, treasuring the feel of her in his arms. "All you need to do is rest."

"But I—"

He silenced her with a gentle kiss. "It doesn't matter," Eric held her gaze. "The only things that matter right now are you and our baby. So I want you to forget everything else. Close your eyes and get some sleep."

"But you—"

He gave her a warning look before pulling the blanket up and around her. Eric watched her take a deep breath. He thought she was going to try and object again. After a moment of hesitation, she rested her head into the small area between his neck and shoulder. It seemed made just for her. He felt her sink into him and he kissed her temple as he stroked her hair. Her breathing deepened and his mind spun, knowing there was going to be a lot to work out. He was going to need help protecting her from it.

His side scorched with each deep breath, but he didn't care. She was in his arms and safe.

That was all that mattered.

Chapter Four

Rebecca stepped out of the shower and looked over the collection of bruises that covered her body. She dried herself off, focused on the welts that covered her abdomen and stomach. Her heart cried in regret as she cradled her stomach protectively. She took a deep breath and forced the *what if's* out of her head.

She looked and felt like a worn punching bag. It felt good to be clean, even if the hot water didn't erase the aches and pains. She donned a fresh hospital gown and a comfortable robe before she stopped looking at her reflection. Her bruises had gone from deep purple to black and green. Just like those on the rest of her body and she sighed in defeat. There was no makeup in the world that could help her now.

Her mind went to Eric. The soft warmth of his arms remained wrapped around her. She would be forever grateful for the angel of a nurse who took her to see him. Being with him had made a world of difference and she felt her strength returning.

Her entire body ached and she honestly felt like she could sleep for a week. She sat on the bed, the distinct smell of bleach tingled her nose. She realized they'd changed the sheets while she was gone. She lay down, her head resting against the pillow. The crisp fibers rubbed roughly against her cheek and she closed her eyes.

Her mind began to roil and a sudden rush of thoughts poured over her. Her body immediately tensed and she opened her eyes. She shifted onto her back and took a breath.

There was a knock at the door before Lucy stepped in with a wide smile. "Hey, Beccs, how are you feeling this morning?"

"I'm good." Rebecca took notice of the shopping bags in her sister's hands. "What's all this?"

"Well, I felt bad about yesterday. So I decided a little shopping was in order." A mischievous grin appeared on her sister's face and Rebecca's stomach knotted. "I borrowed your car. I hope you don't mind. Wait until you see what I found!"

Within half an hour, baby clothes, toys and books covered the bed. Rebecca did her best not to feel overwhelmed when she looked over the array of items. Lucy animatedly talked about each piece and why she had to buy it. Just when she thought it was over, Lucy revealed a second overflowing bag.

Rebecca continued to listen politely to her sister when a crest of nausea began to build in the back of her throat. She pushed it back. She took a few deep breaths and the general discomfort of her body rose. Her neck tingled and she felt the edges of her mouth water while her stomach churned.

"Lucy." The building pressure became unrelenting and Rebecca's brain swam. Not entirely sure she could make it to the bathroom alone, she called her sister's name again, "Lucy."

Her energy quickly depleted. A loud buzz erupted in her ears, drowning out Lucy's voice. Desperate to shake it off, her stomach surged and then clenched. She slid off the bed and ran to the bathroom. She barely made it through the door before she lurched forward, emptying the contents of her stomach into the toilet.

Rebecca's eyes closed as she knelt down. All the veins in her head throbbed, the unimaginable pressure of her body siphoning through them. She leaned on the front of the toilet. Her forehead rested on her arm in sudden exhaustion. She fought against the continued agitation of her stomach.

"Beccs, wait until you see the overalls I bought you." Lucy called from outside the door. "I used one of those pregnancy pillows to try and find the right size. I just had to get them. Oh, and I picked up this pink shirt with little flowers along the collar and it's not too fitted at the bottom and longer so it will . . ."

With a silent thank you that the door closed on its own, she rested her head against the cool tile wall. She waited for the pulsing ache to subside. A hesitant breath spawned panic and her mouth watered before her stomach contracted. She pushed herself over the toilet in defeat.

Her eyes teared and her body shook until the surging expulsion finally stopped. She sat back, but her stomach continued to cramp painfully. An unexplained heaviness pounded against her eyes. She laid her head on her arm, desperate to breathe.

She could hear Lucy fiercely arguing with someone. Rebecca debated whether she was going to be able to move without her stomach revolting. She heard a soft knock on the door.

"Beccs, can I come in?"

The sound of Donna's voice brought a swell of relief and she took in a deep breath. Her mouth began to water again and she whimpered as her stomach spasmed. The door opened as she lost control and lurched over the toilet.

"Beccs, sweetheart."

Her stomach continued to clench in agony and she felt Donna pull back her hair. Her body painfully heaved twice more before the ripples of nausea began to subside. She closed her eyes and sat back. Weakly leaning against Donna, her stomach convulsed and her head felt overwhelmingly heavy on her neck.

"Beccs, do you think you can get up?"

She nodded and Donna helped her off the floor. Rebecca focused on getting her feet to cooperate. Donna walked with her and the nausea began to subside.

"Okay, here we go, nice and slow."

Her head, while still heavy in exhaustion, gradually began to clear. She could take a breath without penalty.

"Here's the shirt I was talking about." Lucy appeared in front of them and Rebecca involuntarily jumped, almost losing her footing.

"Not now, Lucy, we need to get Beccs—"

"Don't tell me what to do!"

"Lucy, she didn't mean—" Rebecca started, her voice weak and brittle as she acknowledged the shivering ache running through her veins.

"Yes, she did," Lucy turned on her heel. "I don't know what you want me to do, Beccs! I thought you would appreciate that I'm excited about the baby! I wanted us to be able to share in the fun . . ."

"It was sweet . . . really." She felt her knees weaken and the bed looked miles away.

"But I guess that's reserved for your mindless minions, who couldn't have an opinion if it bit them in the ass," Lucy threw the various items back into the bags. "So, those of us who choose not to worship the ground you walk on are once again left behind."

"Lucy!" Donna snapped. "Enough!"

"Enough? You're right that's enough."

Rebecca felt someone tug at her arm, throwing her off balance.

"We don't need your help! Let go of her, I'll take it from here!"

"Lucy, please . . ."

"Don, it's okay." Just wanting to get to the bed, Rebecca let Lucy wrap her arm around her waist. They were only a few feet away and there was a knock at the door.

"Go away!" Lucy yelled.

Rebecca winced.

"Come in," Donna said, obviously suppressing her irritation as Rebecca met her eyes.

"Hey, is this a bad time?" Charlie stepped into the room, a tray of coffee in his hands.

"Coffee, that's the last thing she needs."

Rebecca felt her legs disintegrating from beneath her and the conversation faded away in her mind.

"Whoa . . ."

Her eyes slipped close and she felt someone at her back as she leaned.

"Charlie . . ." Donna called from far away.

Rebecca felt the weight of her legs disappear. Her head rested on warmth and she struggled to open her eyes. Starched sheets and the wafting of bleach told her she was back in bed. She heard only mumbling before the surrounding conversation came back into focus.

"Well, I . . ."

Rebecca half-opened her eyes at the sound of Harry's voice.

"These are for the rest of us. I didn't know what to get Rebecca, so I asked Charlie to come up here to ask you what you thought I should get."

"Oh, well, what else do they have?"

Rebecca heard Lucy's voice calm.

"It'll have to be something decaffeinated, of course."

"Of course."

Rebecca couldn't help but covertly smirk in her own mind.

"But I really don't know what Beccs likes and I don't want

to get the wrong thing. Wait, do you think you could come with me? It will only take a second."

"Are you going to be okay for a few minutes without me, Beccs?"

Lucy's voice puller her out of the warmth.

"Beccs?"

"Charlie and I will stay with her, she'll be fine," Donna said.

Rebecca was quietly thankful for not having to remember how to talk.

"Okay, let's make it quick. Oh, wait until you see what I . . ."

Their voices faded again and she let herself relax in the quiet settling around her. A gentle hand smoothed back her hair as the blankets pulled over her. She released herself into the darkness, drifting away into slumber.

The pain pills kicked in and he called Adam. Eric knew his partner was doing everything he could to delay the onslaught of police. He wanted to check in and get a timetable.

"Stiles, you're alive!"

"Yeah, for now anyway."

"I swear, you have more lives than an alley cat."

"I'll take that as a compliment. Thanks for holding back the dogs."

"Not a problem, there's enough evidence outside the hospital to keep everyone busy for a while."

"How much longer do you think it's going to last?"

"I can give you another six to eight hours. After that we're going to have a problem."

"Understood." He took a breath, Rebecca's fragile form stamped in his mind. "Adam, I need your help."

"Sure, anything."

Eric proceeded to explain the situation with Rebecca and the baby. As well as his concerns about what would happen next.

"I'll take care of it."

It was a simple statement but in it, Eric knew he had nothing to worry about.

There was a knock at the door and he stashed the phone just beneath the blanket before he called the person into the room.

"Hey, brother, you're looking better," Charlie greeted with a smile.

"I'm alive. You look like you made it through relatively unscathed."

"My tactical skills do come in handy from time to time. How are you feeling?"

"According to the doctors, I could pull apart at the seams in any given moment. Besides that, I'm sore but good."

"Have you seen Beccs?"

"Yeah, I saw her last night . . . this morning . . . earlier." A hesitant sigh escaped his chest.

"She told you what the doctor said?"

"Yeah, lots of rest, no stress." Eric nodded, looking to Charlie. "I want to get her out of here while we still can. Adam is stalling for the moment, but it's not going to last forever."

"I don't know if that is such a good idea."

"Why? She said she's feeling better."

"She's trying and last night she probably felt like she could go another hundred laps, but I don't think we're out of the woods yet." Charlie dug his hands in his pockets. He met Eric's eyes with concern. "Her adrenaline was pushing her along pretty good last night. Now that her body's had time to settle, that's going to change fairly fast. Unfortunately, I don't think the worst has hit yet."

"How is she now?" Eric reminded himself to breathe.

"Lucy was helping her when I got there and she was really weak. I ended up carrying her back to bed. She fell asleep as soon as I laid her down and Donna said she found her in the bathroom, nauseous."

"Who's with her now?"

"Donna. Dad is keeping Lucy occupied for the moment so she can sleep. Don't know how long that's going to last though."

"Yeah," Eric's thoughts spun. "Probably not long enough."

"What's Lucy's deal anyway?"

"Why, did something happen?"

"Not really. She just seems a little . . ."

"Unbalanced?"

"Uh, yeah, I guess."

"Lucy is carrying a lot of baggage. While I'm thankful that she's here, she has a tendency to dump unneeded crap on Beccs. Obviously, that is the last thing she needs right now."

"Understood, no problem," Charlie replied with an accepting nod. "I'll make sure everything stays mellow until you're on your feet. How long before they let you out?"

"I'm pushing for tomorrow."

"Good luck with that."

"Thanks. Charlie, I . . ."

"Yeah?"

"Thanks for being my brother and saving my ass."

"There's no one else's ass I'd rather save, brother. That's what family's for, right?"

Rebecca groggily looked around the room through unfocused eyes and made a mental note that she didn't see any sign of Lucy. Her eyes slid close, a murmur of nausea rumbled and then subsided as her whole body ached.

Able to focus as the gray of sleep lifted, her lids rose. She saw Harry next to her bed, reading a magazine and she couldn't help but smile. "Is it at least a good article?"

He looked over with a grin. "Nah, but it was better than the liberal ranting of *Time*," he closed the magazine and sat forward in his chair. "Welcome back."

"I didn't know I was gone." The last thing she remembered was Donna helping her back to bed after her meeting with the toilet. "How long have I been asleep?"

"A couple hours."

"Did I scare everyone away?"

"Nope, they just went to get some food."

"Are they bringing some back for me?"

"I don't know, but I'll tell you what, if they don't, we can share mine."

"I think I can live with that." Her heart warmed at the sight of him. She pushed her hand beneath the pillow, rolling onto her side. "Have you seen Eric?"

"A little while ago, yes."

"How is he?"

"Ah well, he's stubborn, frustrated and going stir crazy," he replied with a shrug and a smile. "Besides that, he's fine."

"Harry, I know that he's worried, but . . . don't let him hurt himself. I don't want him . . ."

"Rebecca, I learned a long time ago that he's going to do what he's going to do. There's nothing you or I or anyone else can do about it."

"I suppose you're right and he says I'm stubborn."

Harry released a small chuckle of amusement. "You seem like you're feeling better."

"I guess I am."

She sat up just as the door opened and Donna entered the room with an armful of bags.

"Hey, sweetie, you're awake!"

"You brought food!"

"Chili cheese fries."

"Really?"

"Yep."

"Yum." Rebecca shifted out of the bed and Harry rose to help her. She took his hand as she slipped her feet onto the floor. The tie of her robe came loose and she tightened it and headed to the bathroom.

Her stomach growled in hunger. She couldn't wait to dig into her chili cheese fries. They were her favorite indulgence and she hoped that the baby would enjoy them as well. Either way, she guessed she was going to find out.

She closed the door, disappearing within the bathroom. She washed her hands and pulled a towel from the rack above the toilet. Something caught her eye and she looked closer. It was a smear of blood and her heart stopped.

Her entire body shook in fear, her heart thudding loudly in her ears. She told her legs to move. The air ripped through her lungs. She gripped the handle of the door. It opened and she heard the chattering of happy voices. She stepped out and faced a room full of people. Before she even had a chance to react, Lucy slammed into her, wrapping her in a hug.

"I was so worried!"

Rebecca felt the color drain from her cheeks. Her terror besieged her and the room became a muffled blur.

Eric . . .

The baby . . .

Our baby.

Her mind moved in slow motion. Lucy's excited voice swirled around her as the laughing and chatter of her friends deafened her ears. She felt trapped and fearfully searched with blind eyes for a glint of knowing. For someone who could hear her screaming. Her entire body tightened in terror as she gasped for air. Then she saw Harry.

She met his eyes. A look of realization crossed his face. He moved and a light of hope shined.

The baby . . .

Frantic, she tried to free herself from Lucy's grasp.

Pain smacked at her, cutting her in half. The force instantaneously crippled her. She gasped and cried out as she curled into herself. Her hand clenched her stomach and she fell forward. Her free hand landed on the linoleum as her knees hit the ground.

God please . . . no . . . please no . . .

She pushed away the terror. Her eyes closed in a desperate attempt to make the pain disappear. Everything rushed back into focus, panic hitting her hard in the chest as she tried to breathe. Hands pressed on her arms and someone called her name. She opened her eyes and saw Harry.

"Can you put your arms around my neck?"

She tried to hang on to his shoulders and he swept her off the floor. Her body tensed in anticipation, her heart threatening to pound out of her chest. She felt the steady stream of tears sliding down her cheeks. She hid her face in his shoulder.

He laid her on the bed and she reached out, easing herself down. A bursting pain clutched her abdomen. Unable to hold it back, she cried out as it surged through her. Her entire body felt like it was going to shatter.

"Rebecca . . ."

She heard from somewhere beyond the agony.

"Rebecca, sweetheart, look at me."

Someone gripped her hand and she opened her eyes. Harry smiled at her and her heart ached.

"I know it hurts, but you need to breathe."

He did his best to console her, but another surge of agony racked her body and she sobbed in misery and terror. "The baby . . ." she cried through broken breaths, begging for help.

"Come on, Rebecca, you need to tap into that fire and fight now. You need to hang on."

"Harry . . ." she gasped, struggling against her own body.

"I know you're scared, but you need to breathe. You need to focus and push the pain away."

His words were far away and her body wept as she waited for the next assault to rage through her.

"You can do it."

The pain ripped her in half and she could only see a blinding white light, hearing herself scream. The peak finally crested and started to slide and she tried to take a breath, her eyes with Harry.

"That's it, deep breaths."

"Eric," her heart sobbed.

"He's coming," he said, desperate reassurance in his eyes, but the agony coursed through her again and she curled into her knees. "Just hang on."

Eric finished his tenth lap down the hall and felt good. The nurse had gotten him a pair of pajama bottoms. It was agreed that if he could do a dozen laps without popping any of his stitches, she would take him down to see Rebecca.

His thoughts swirled around the future and he recognized the light of hope she'd ignited within him. The prospect of a family had never been a prevalent thing in his mind, but now . . .

He was excited.

He adored the way she smiled when she told him about the baby. Her entire body glowed in happiness and he knew he'd had a part in that. The silly picture of a blob within a blob, but what that little blob was becoming, growing inside her beautiful body. The thought of it was staggering and humbling at the same time.

He turned with a smile, reaching the end of the hall. Eric stopped in confusion seeing Charlie race toward him, terror in his eyes.

Beccs.

Eric ripped the IV from his arm. He moved as quickly as he could, meeting Charlie in front of the elevator. There was no need for words, he knew what was happening. He heard the nurse yelling at him to stop when the doors of the elevator closed. He took a breath, the doors opened and he followed Charlie down the hall.

He immediately saw Donna and Lucy, looking grief stricken and pale.

Then he heard her scream.

Eric pushed through the door as a team of doctors and nurses moved frantically around the room. In the middle of it was Rebecca sobbing in pain as she clung to his father's hand.

Eric moved around the bed as a nurse pulled an oxygen mask over Rebecca's face. His eyes remained on her. He put a hand on his father's shoulder, Harry moved and he reached out taking her hand.

"You need to get her to breathe," he heard his dad say before he disappeared into the blur behind him.

Tears streamed from beneath her tightly shut eyes. His heart shattered and he froze. She was in such overwhelming pain and he didn't know what to do. Everything slowed, his heart pounding loudly against his chest. It was his worst nightmare and a crushing helplessness overpowered reason, leaving him completely paralyzed.

Without warning, she curled in agony. A screaming sob fell from her lips and she gripped his hand tightly.

She needs you.

. . . and now there are all these things I want, because of her . . .

Snapping himself out of his self-induced trance, he immediately refocused. "Beccs, I'm here," he called to her over the noise of the room as she continued to sob. "Beccs, baby, look at me."

Eric moved against the bed in an effort to get closer to her. Out of the way of the medical team, he took position at the head of the bed. His hand went into her hair as his thumb caressed her temple.

"Rebecca, open your eyes and look at me," he called, hovering next to her as he continued to stroke her hair. Her eyes opened and his heart spiked in pain, when she started to cry again. "Sweetheart, look at me, stay with me."

She struggle to focus on him through her torment. He touched her cheek, locking the liquid of her eyes, seeing them call to him in fear.

"Stay right here," he said, giving her a small nod. "Now take a breath."

She closed her eyes.

He watched her inhale and then exhale before her eyes opened to look at him again. "Again," he said and she repeated the process. "That's right, let's do it again."

She took a deep breath and her grip tightened around his hand. The surrounding monitors beeped wildly and she tensed in gasping agony.

"Rebecca, stay with me," he said, his voice demanding. "Beccs, look at me."

Her head arched back into the pillow. She suppressed a scream as he held onto her and then watched her twist her body inward.

"Do something!" he growled in trembling rage, fiercely looking to the group of nurses and doctors that worked around them before focusing back on Rebecca.

"Sweetheart, open your eyes," he said as he leaned into her ear curbing his frustration. "Look at me. I need you to stay with me."

Her beautiful blue eyes stared back at him and he smiled in reassurance.

"Hey, beautiful, take a deep breath for me," he said as he stroked her cheek, watching the mask clear and then fog as she did as he asked. "Good girl, keep going. I love you so much."

Eric smiled down at her and she took another breath on her own. He kept her eyes within his as he kissed her hand. Her hold tightened around his hand and her eyes rolled back.

"Rebecca, look at me, baby. You can do this, stay with me." The noise around him instantly went up three decimals. Her hand went limp as her eyes closed.

"*Rebecca*," he exclaimed, holding her face in his hands. "Beccs, please. Baby, open your eyes . . . What happened? Help her!"

Told to get off the bed, Eric's heart quickly sunk and stopped beating. "Do something!"

"Sir, we're doing everything we can. I need you to step back."

"Where are you taking her?"

"Surgery."

"What's happening? What's wrong?"

"Sir, she's losing the baby and we think your wife's bleeding internally."

"Can you stop it? What are you going to do?"

"Everything we can."

"What does—"

"I can't talk to you right now, sir. I need to get her into surgery. I'll send out news as soon as I can, I promise."

He was completely breathless as he watched her leave. He moved mindlessly, stepping back until he hit the wall. The room was deathly silent. The white walls glared at him as he slid down in disbelief. He clung to her eyes as he pushed it away, unbelieving that he would never see them again.

They're going to make it through this.

His mind became a whirl of images he was unable to fight off. He saw his father looking back at him from the doorway. His normally calm pleasant eyes were red and heavy. He waited for him to say something encouraging or hopeful. There was nothing, just empty silence. Eric wallowed in it, pulled it in as a cushion. He drowned in it, so that all that remained were her eyes and her smile.

CHAPTER FIVE

Soft fingers brushed through her hair. Warmth enveloped her and she sighed in contentment. Her thoughts began to lift, but then hesitated as pain tugged at her. A shrouded emptiness suppressed her heart. She could see Eric, his face filled with pain and worry as he talked to her.

Stay with me, Beccs . . . focus on me . . .

All around him was unbelievable pain. It paralyzed her and she couldn't breathe.

Breathe Beccs. Take a deep breath.

"That's our baby."

"And what's the black?"

"My uterus."

"Ah, that makes sense, so you're both okay?"

Oh god . . . no . . . please no . . .

The baby.

Please no . . .

The ache grew inside her as her chest tightened.

"Shhh, Beccs . . . I'm here, baby . . . I'm here . . ."

His arms tightened around her protectively. His warmth surrounded her, the gentle smell of his skin caressed her senses as his soft hand slid over her cheek.

Our baby.

Her conscious lifted beyond her control. She rose into the pain and it quickly consumed her. Her heart ripped as hot tears rolled down her cheeks.

Our baby's gone . . . oh god I killed our baby . . . please . . .

Please, it can't be true . . . don't let it be true . . . I love our ba-

by . . . please don't . . .

She felt him pull her into his chest. She gripped at his shirt as her heart continued to throb in torment and her entire body wept.

"Beccs, please come back to me."

I can't . . . it hurts too much . . . please make it stop . . . please . . .

"Sweetheart, I'm here . . . I need you. Please, Beccs . . ."

"Eric . . ." She breathed quietly into his chest. His arms tightened around her before he kissed the top of her head. "The baby's gone."

"Yes," he replied in a shaken whisper.

Her heart clenched again in agony. "I'm so sorry," she said, pushing through her tears.

"No." His hand wrapped in her hair before she felt him move. "Beccs, look at me."

She kept her eyes closed as guilt rolled through her. Her heart screamed and she refused to look at the disappointment in his eyes.

"Rebecca, open your eyes and look at me." His voice was gentle and filled with emotion. "Beccs, please . . ."

She lifted her eyes and found him intently watching. His eyes were red and wet with tears.

"This was not your fault," he said, his voice cracking as his eyes both pierced and cradled her heart. "You didn't do anything wrong, baby. It wasn't your fault."

"Why did this happen?" she asked him as tears slid down her cheeks. She tried to move and winced in shooting pain. "I should've known I . . . I'm so sorry, Eric . . ."

"Sweetheart, no," he pleaded, his breath wet with emotion as he held her tightly and she cried onto his shoulder. "It wasn't your fault. There was nothing you could've done."

"I'm so sorry."

"I'm not going to let you blame yourself for this, baby. It

wasn't your fault, it wasn't anybody's fault."

She searched his eyes, his face, looking for any sign of disappointment or doubt. She only saw love and worry.

"It's awful and I know it hurts, but I need you to hang on. We're going to get through this. I promise it's going to be okay."

Every piece of him seemed to plead with her to hear him. She bit back the guilt that wasn't going to fade. She slowly nodded and he kissed her temple. Her arms curled around his neck, pulling him close and she tried to breathe.

"I love you, Rebecca. I love you so much," he said, his breath heavy.

"I love you, too."

Her breath escaped her as the tears fell. Her heart overflowed with intense, aching love as she held him. He was so amazing, incredibly strong and full of life. She knew she didn't deserve him. She'd put him through so much and yet here he was still holding her tightly.

Why is he still here?

I've hurt him so much . . .

Ashamed that she'd been so helpless and weak, guilt once again breathed through her. A constant tapping against her heart, it pushed out little whispers of anguished remorse that slid and pooled in the bottom of her stomach.

Her body aching, she hid herself in his chest, his arms snuggly encircling her. Rebecca closed her eyes and focused on the rhythm of his heart against her cheek. The tears continued to fall as her chest throbbed and her body wept. The cocoon of his arms surrounded her and she felt loved and protected. She drifted into the rise and fall of his chest. The gentle brush of his hands in her hair, she slowly felt her mind float away.

Her mind rose into conscious thought and as her eyes opened. She prepared for the devastating anguish to punch at her heart. Deeply inhaling air into her body, there was a pang in the back of her throat that resonated through her at a constant hum. Everything else was numb, hollow and un-affected. Somehow separated from the raw torment, she could still feel it buzzing beneath her skin.

A still constant warmth around her, she savored it as she lifted her eyes. His strong sculpted face was turned down slightly as if he'd rested his cheek on her head. Deep in slumber, she gently grazed the scruff of his chin with her fingertips.

He was in a light blue set of scrubs, an IV line still at-tached to the inside of his wrist. She wondered if he was in pain and how uncomfortable laying in the bed on his side was. She also knew how stubborn he was and that he wouldn't have cared.

Her head curled back into his chest. She wanted to let him rest. She wanted to soothe him as he soothed her. She wasn't the only one hurting.

Her thoughts trailed back. Hesitation in saying the words even within the comfort of her own mind. Lightly tracing the creases in his shirt, she thought about him opening his eyes. His voice in her ear. The feel of his hand as it caressed her cheek. She wondered if now it was all going to change.

Would she see the same gleaming warmth in his gaze or had she extinguished it?

He insisted it wasn't her fault. She could see the intensity of his eyes as he pleaded for her to believe him. She'd nod-ded in comfort to him, her heart knowing the truth.

It was her fault, she should have known.

She let him down.

She should've done more to protect their baby.

Her forehead against his chest, she abruptly felt the soft caress of his hand. Lithe fingers on the back of her neck, they gently massaged the tension away. She didn't move, letting his strong hand continue to knead the strained muscles until it drifted over her spine resting comfortably on the small of her back.

Her eyes lifted to meet his and she found him waiting. His gaze glassed with deep worry, he brushed his fingers through her hair. He shifted with a grimace and she reached out in concern as he lowered himself down the bed.

Lying face to face on the pillow, her hand caressed his cheek. He closed his eyes as she traced the line of his jaw.

"I'm sorry," she said, her voice just above a whisper and he pushed his hand into her hair, his thumb feathering against her temple.

"I don't want to ever hear you say that," he replied gently, his eyes staying within hers. "There's nothing to be sorry for."

"Yes there is," she replied as she nodded, her hand resting on his chest." I wasn't strong enough." She saw him start to object and gently covered his mouth with her index finger. "We lost our . . ." she started, her voice cracking as she was unable to utter the words. "I haven't been here for you. I know how much you wanted . . ."

"Shhh, Beccs, stop," he said, moving closer to her as she held back the water edging her eyes. "We're in this together."

"But I . . ."

"Sweetheart, you never left me," he reassured with a small smile. "You've been here with me the whole time. Being able to hold you has done wonders for my heart."

"Liar."

"Never," he replied as his thumb caressed her cheek. He pulled her close, leaning forward to place a gentle kiss on her lips. "You're all I need."

CHAPTER SIX

"She seems to be handling this pretty well, all things con-sidered," Adam commented as Eric went through his mail.

A little too well . . .

He was off duty, but both he and Rebecca were asked to come to the station to review their statements. She'd been in with the interviewing officer for a few hours now and Adam offered to check in on her.

They'd taken it a moment at a time. Some were harder to get through than others. While he'd thought they'd gotten through the worst of it, now he wasn't as sure. They'd released her from the hospital first, just hours after she woke in his arms. The plan was to have Donna stay with her at the house. Eric found out a few days later that Lucy had muscled her way in, insisting that Rebecca needed family to support her, not friends.

It was when he got home that he started to notice it. She was quiet and withdrawn. The sparkle from her eyes had disappeared. Yet to the naked eye, she was fine. There were no signs of depression or moodiness. She was just . . . flat, as if all the fiery passion had been extinguished. He wasn't sure what to do or if he should even consider it a problem.

"How are you doing?"

"Good, pain meds help," Eric replied with a smirk.

Adam looked away with a smile. "And Rebecca?"

"She's okay. Taking it a day at a time," he replied with a nod as he continued to shift through the stack of paper in front of him. "It's hard, but we're getting through."

"Let me know if you need anything," Adam offered. "When you guys are ready and things settle down a little, Olivia wants you to come to the house for dinner."

"That sounds great. I know Beccs will be happy to meet her," Eric replied.

When they arrived at the station that morning, he'd been talking himself down. If things got rough, he knew he couldn't step in and protect her. As it would make things so much worse. She needed to give her statement uninfluenced by him or anyone else. Without it, they would have no case against Gregorn, a.k.a. the slime trying to purchase her.

"Have you guys talked about what happened at all?"

"Not yet," he replied with a deep breath. "I don't want to push her."

"Eric," Adam started until a breath of hesitation sounded. "I know that you want to give her space, but . . ."

"But?"

"I've seen the transcripts and there are a few things that have come up. Specifically about the locket."

"What about the locket?"

"It's missing again."

"What?"

"According to Rebecca's statement, she was the last one to have it."

"You've got to be freaking kidding me," Eric said. Heaviness settled in his chest as he struggled against the twisting in his gut. "This is unbelievable."

The door opened again and she watched her interrogator enter the room and take a seat across the table.

She was strong . . . she was done being a weeping, withering fool.

She could handle this.

"I apologize for the interruption," he offered.

She straightened her back, preparing for the next attack.

"Let's move on, shall we?"

"Sure."

"I wanted to ask you about Kevin Ivey."

"I'm sorry, who?"

"The man you shot at the airport," he said.

She refused to react to it. "You have a question?"

"Can you tell me again, what happened?"

"Sure. I . . . uh . . . Eric had just shot Gregorn. I got up to run when I saw him coming out of the shadows to my right. He had his . . . he had his gun aimed at Er . . . Detective Stiles. I tried to warn him, but it was too late."

"Then what happened?"

"I went to check Detective Stile's wound. I unwrapped him from his vest and began putting pressure on the wound until I could get help."

"The detective was bleeding badly?"

"Yes."

"Did you know at that moment where his gun was?"

"No. I don't think so . . . no."

"Please continue."

"I was trying to slow the bleeding and a man approached me. He had a gun and told me to get up. I refused."

"Was that man Kevin Ivey?"

"Yes."

"Are you sure?"

"Yes."

"What happened then?"

"I told him that he was going to have to kill me to get me to move. He then . . . he picked me up off the ground and started . . . he tried to pull me away. I saw the gun on the ground. I fought against him and broke free, but he . . . that was when . . . that was . . ."

She broke free from his grasp, grabbed for the weapon, spun and fired. The bullet hit square in the chest and he looked at her in disbelief. She stepped back in shock as he fell. She dropped the gun as the world paused for a moment.

She told her body to take a breath and then it complied.

She pulled back into herself for a moment as she turned back to the table, allowing her the comfort of Eric's eyes and smile, the feel of his arms around her as she melted against him.

She was doing this for him, for them.

She didn't want to be the needy girlfriend, the fragile woman protected and sheltered by her strong man. That wasn't fair to him, he deserved someone who could take care of herself and wasn't going to crumble at the first sign of pressure. She used to be that person. She used to be able to kick ass and take names. She used to not need the shelter of someone's arms to make her feel safe and now . . .

"Ms. Gailen . . . Rebecca?"

The sound of her name pulled her from her mind and she looked to him in embarrassment. "I'm sorry, did you ask me something?"

"No. I uh . . ." he started and then stumbled. "You were telling me about what happened with Kevin Ivey. Ivey grabbed you. You broke free and then what happened?"

"I shot him."

It was the truth.

She shot him square in the chest.

She killed him.

"Okay, Rebecca, let's talk about the locket."

"What about it?" she asked, thrown by the topic of discussion.

"Where was the last place you saw it?"

"I, uh . . . I guess it would have been when Valnes wrapped it around my neck before we left the estate."

"So he put it on you," he verified. "Do you know why he did that?"

"To be an ass? I honestly don't know."

"Do you remember ever taking it off?"

"No."

"And when did you realize it was no longer around your neck?"

"Ah, well . . . to be honest I didn't notice until I got home a few days ago. With everything that happened, it slipped my mind."

"That's a pretty big thing to forget, don't you think?"

"No, not under the circumstances."

"And what were the circumstances exactly?" he asked.

She couldn't believe he was actually asking her to recount what happened at the hospital. "Eric had been shot, so we were taken to the hospital."

"We, who's we?"

"Eric, myself and Charlie, his brother."

"Didn't I see Detective Stiles in the hallway?"

"Yes, he's here as well."

"And what is your relationship?"

"We're involved."

"Involved?"

"He's my boyfriend, we live together."

"So you were worried."

"Yes, of course."

"But he's fine, so there had to be something else to distract you."

"What do you want from me?"

"Like I said, just looking for the truth."

"I don't know what happened to it. As far as I was told, everything I was wearing was put into a bag with the rest of my clothes."

"The burgundy dress?"

"Yes."

"We checked. It wasn't there."

"I don't know what to tell you," she replied, giving him an even stare. "Are we finished?"

"For now." He rose from the table and she followed. "We'll call if we need anything else."

"I have no doubt."

Rebecca walked down the hallway toward Eric's desk. She slowed her pace, trying to rein in her emotions before she saw him. He was concerned about her having to do the interview so soon after . . . everything.

She needed to show him that she could handle it. That she was fine. He didn't need to worry about her anymore. She could take care of herself and anyone else who came along as well. Not only was she a proud cop's girlfriend, but she was a tough girlfriend who could stand beside him instead of behind him.

She could do this . . .

She turned the corner to see his desk was empty. She released a held breath and moved a little quicker. She grabbed a post it and a pen to leave him a note.

"Hey, beautiful."

She turned and he wrapped her in his arms. She found his adoring beautiful eyes shining back at her. The warmth of him cascaded through her and he leaned down brushing her lips with a loving kiss.

"Are you all done?"

"Yep."

"Everything's okay?" He brushed his fingers through her hair.

She had to stop her eyes from closing.

"You're okay?"

"Glad it's over."

"Yeah, me, too," he searched her eyes.

She struggled to keep them calm and bright.

"Are you ready to head home?"

"If you can, you don't have to stay, do you?"

"Nope, I am all yours." He pulled her closer with a greedy look.

"Stiles."

Eric's chin dropped. "Yes, sir," Eric's arms released her and moved toward the man calling him.

"I need you and Adam in my office." The man stopped, looking at Rebecca. "Ms. Gailen."

Not sure what to say, she nodded in respect and he disappeared around the corner.

Eric turned to her, disappointment in his eyes. "I have to go." He grasped her hand with a sigh. "I'm sorry, Beccs."

"It's fine. I can wait."

"No, I don't know how long it's going to take and you need to rest."

"It's fine."

"Here are the keys to the truck. Go home and I'll just have Adam drop me off when we're done."

"Okay."

"I'll see you when I get home."

A bellowing voice came from the hallway.

"I love you."

Kissing her, he pulled away, flashing a smile before disappearing down the hall.

Rebecca looked down at the keys in her hands. She debated if she should just wait or go home. She didn't mind waiting, but it may look like she couldn't stand to be away from him, so she chose to go home.

Her mind was tired and heavy. She decided she wanted to soak in a hot bath and then crawl into bed. She pulled into the driveway and heard the reverberating sound of a thumping bass.

The blaring music thudded, making the door vibrate when she opened the front door.

Rebecca dropped her purse on the couch. She moved across the room hitting the power button on the stereo. As soon as she did, she regretted it, hearing her sister and another nameless person grunting from the spare room. A line of discarded clothing led to the bedroom and kicking the clothing as she went, she piled it in front of Lucy's door.

She cleared miscellaneous garbage off the island and put the milk back in the fridge. Wiping down the counter and taking out the garbage, she walked in from the garage to see Lucy. Rebecca pushed her hair behind her ear, fixing the pillows on the couch.

"Hey, Beccs, when did you get home?"

"A little while ago."

"Where's Eric?"

"At the station."

"Figures." Lucy took a sip of her water. "They always disappear when things get bad."

Rebecca crossed the room, headed to her own bedroom.

"And you're going to just let him do it." Rebecca stopped and turned to face her. "That got your attention."

"Please stop."

"Why? Am I upsetting you?"

"What's going on?"

"I want my sister back."

"I'm right here."

"You've changed."

"I haven't—"

"Yes, you have! You've turned into this weepy, fragile little girlfriend who will do whatever her big, strong man tells her to and I'm sick of watching him control you!"

"It has nothing to do with Eric."

"So what's your deal? You're walking around here like a goddamn zombie!"

"Stop, Lucy." Rebecca turned away.

"You were pregnant for a whole eight hours. Get over it, Beccs!"

She shut the door to her room, pushing her sister's words away.

Rebecca ignored her thumping heart, turned the faucet and started the water for a nice, long bath. She tried to ignore her plethora of bruises beneath her clothes. They'd gone from a black violet to a lighter purple, tinged with a greenish yellow. The bruising around her incision was still dark purple. The swelling had gone down and the stitches were slowly disappearing. She allowed herself to look at them once a day. Otherwise, the memories would flood her and she couldn't control the emotion that accompanied them.

She turned off the water and slid into the steaming delight of the tub. She immersed herself in the warmth and closed her eyes. She'd tried to relax since she got home but found it difficult. It was as if someone had turned on her inner alarms and forgot to turn them off. Every little noise, creak or rustle sent her muscles into spasms of fear.

She tried to push the fear away and Lucy's comments fell into her mind.

You were pregnant for a whole eight hours . . . get over it . . .

Was she being too sensitive, blowing it all out of proportion? Did she have the right to be sad? It was a shocking revelation but one that filled her with hope in a bad situation. After everything, it was such a miracle, a sign that there was hope for their future. She'd clung to it, hung her faith on it, as a promise that they would have a life after the nightmare. Then it disappeared.

She rose out of the bathtub and dried off. She changed into a clean t-shirt and boxers before folding down the covers on the bed. She heard her phone ring and went to her purse seeing Eric's name. "Hey, hero."

"Hey, beautiful. Whatchadoin'?"

"Nothing, just got out of the bathtub."

"Sounds like fun."

"Not nearly as much as if you were here. Are you on your way home?"

"Unfortunately, no," he replied.

Her heart sunk a little.

"I'm going to be stuck here for a while longer."

"Um . . . okay," she said, her hand pushing through her hair.

"I'll be home as soon as I can."

She could tell by his tone that he was holding something back.

"Be safe."

"I love you."

"I love you, too." The call ended and she dropped the phone back in her purse.

Rebecca walked back to the bed and curled into herself as she lay down. She turned the lamp on the bedside table off and sunk back into the pillow, taking note of how sore her body still was.

A slow ache had begun to grow since she'd left the station and she wanted him to come home sooner rather than later. She knew full well that the thought was needy and weak. At that particular moment, she didn't care. She missed him and she wasn't going to push that feeling away.

CHAPTER SEVEN

Eric crept into the bedroom and found her sleeping. Closing the door, he moved around the bed, stripped down to changed. Climbing into the bed, he spooned up behind her, the warmth of her body calming him. He breathed her in as he draped his arm over her hip and felt her body tense. She rolled onto her back and her sleepy eyes looked up at him with a smile.

"I'm sorry, baby. I didn't mean to wake you," he said, kissing her forehead.

"I missed you."

He saw an unexpected wetness in her eyes.

She curled into his chest as if hiding from whatever had upset her.

He looked down at her beautiful face as it relaxed against him. "I missed you, too." His arm around her, his fingers trailed up and down her spine while he tried to get his mind to slow.

He hated to see her upset and guilt washed over him about staying late at the station. She was still recovering from what happened. Whether she would admit it or not, he needed to be there to help her through it.

He wasn't supposed to go back to work for another week, but he didn't want to wait to get this resolved. He wanted it to be over. He wanted them to move on.

Loose ends, like the locket, would prevent that from happening. It was the only thing that was pulling him away and he wasn't sure what to do. His eyes closed to the steady rhythm of her breathing. He debated his next move. He needed to find the locket, sooner rather than later.

His mind settled into itself and he drifted off into a light, restless sleep.

His conscience lifted out of the cocoon of sleep. Eric opened his eyes to find her still within his arms. The light in the room had changed, shining an orange glow against the walls. He guessed it was early morning. He glanced at the clock and saw it was a little after six a.m. He watched her sleep. His thumb stroked her temple. He was worried about her.

Beccs is used to taking care of herself and everyone else. She's not used to anyone taking care of her. She thinks it makes her weak . . .

He remembered the night Donna had told him that. Little did he know how accurate the statement would be. He didn't know how to show her that her leaning on him was not a sign of weakness. It was a sign of being human. He wanted her to lean on him. He wanted her to need him, even if it was just a little.

It terrified him that in an effort to be strong, she was going to do more damage than good. He'd seen her try to suppress her anxiety and pain before, not liking the results. She sighed and he focused on her eyes. They fluttered open before looking up at him with a smile.

"Good morning," she reached up, caressing his cheek.

"Morning," her face became contemplative as she studied him. "I missed you last night."

"I'm sorry." He brushed a lingering kiss over her soft lips.

"That's okay, you can make it up to me today," she said, curling her fingers into his hair.

"No, I can't."

"Why?" She looked back to him in confusion.

"I need to go to the station and take care of a few loose

ends."

"You didn't take care of them last night?"

"Yes and no." His arm wrapped around her in an unconscious need to keep her close.

"What's going on?"

"Nothing for you to worry about." She shifted from beneath him in obvious irritation. "Beccs."

"What?"

"You have enough—"

She lifted the blankets off her legs and got out of bed. "Just don't."

"Don't what? Don't dump a lot of unneeded crap in your lap?"

"That's not what I meant."

"Then what?" His frustration with the conversation was confusing. He didn't understand what they were arguing about, but he was glad they were arguing.

"When did you start censoring what we can and cannot talk about?"

"I don't—"

"Yes, you do." The lack of emotion in her voice evident and frustrating him even more.

"I'm not censoring anything."

"Fine." She disappeared into the bathroom.

He followed. "Beccs." He watched her putting toothpaste on her toothbrush. "I didn't think it was anything you needed to be worried about."

"You know part of being honest is not holding back, Eric!"

"Forgive me for trying to protect you!"

"I don't need your protection!"

"I know that. I never said . . ." The fire in her eyes grew as she defended herself to him.

She was fighting him.

His Beccs was coming back.

"I'm not some fragile flower you have to treat with kid gloves! I can handle your life, my life and everything that comes with it, or I wouldn't be here!"

"Okay, I'm sorry. I know you can handle whatever it is that comes into our lives," he admitted with a deep breath, understanding why she was upset. "I didn't mean to become a hovering, overprotective guy, I swear."

"Well you did." Her expression change as if surprised by her own sudden passion.

"I'm sorry. I just don't want you to get overwhelmed. You're still recovering, sweetheart."

"Eric . . ."

"Okay, fine . . . fine. I'll stop. I know that you can handle it. I forgot that you are my tough-as-nails, fiery redhead."

"Don't do it again."

He lessened the gap between them and her eyes softened.

"It's annoying and I don't like being mad at you."

"I don't like it when you're mad at me." His hands enveloped her waist, he pulled her close and her arms looped around his chest.

"How are you feeling?"

"Fine, a little sore." he replied before planting a tender kiss on her lips.

"You know you're supposed to be resting," she whispered into his lips before pressing her lips back to his.

He walked her back.

She sat against the bathroom counter.

"Intriguing and what would resting include exactly?" Eric leaned, breathing against her neck before trailing a line up to just behind her ear. Kissing the tender area, he savored her, his hands caressing the lines of her back.

"Well, there would be steamy showers, hours of languidly lying in bed, hot-oil massages . . ."

"Massages?"

"Of course, didn't you know I took a masseur class in college?"

He grazed at her ribs with his fingertips. His lips pressed against her collarbone.

"I've been told my hands are ethereal and demonic at the same time."

"Sounds exotic." Her nails skimmed the back of his neck, sending chills up his spine, her legs trapping his waist.

"Exotic enough for you to stay home?"

"Maybe." He met her gaze before devouring her lips. He pulled her off the counter and walked her back into the bedroom.

She tugged at his shirt and pushed it over his head.

Her nails sent tingles through his body as they slid down his chest. His mouth continued its heady consumption of her lips.

They reached the bed and supporting her back, he lowered her beneath him. Her arms danced around his waist as his fingers pushed into her hair. His mouth nipped at her ear before trailing down her neck. His hands began to push her shirt up when he heard his cell phone ring.

He began to kiss every bump and bruise covering her beautiful body. Each discolored mark reminding him of what it felt like almost to lose her. The emotion attached to the memory was overwhelming. He rose back up, taking her face in his hands.

"I love you, Beccs." Eric wrapped his arms around her before covering her mouth with deep, enduring kisses. The splendor of her arms around him made him want nothing more than to hold her beneath him forever.

His phone rang again. He ignored it, letting it go to voicemail. His focus remained on her soft body beneath his hands.

The phone rang a third time and it got his attention. He lifted his mouth as she lined his lower lip with the tip of her finger. Still debating, he leaned down to kiss her when the phone rang again. He groaned in protest as he rolled off the bed and grabbed it off the dresser.

Eric dialed his voicemail and sat on the bed as she came up behind him. Her arms draped over his shoulders as she kissed his neck. The voicemail was from Adam. Some additional information came in about the locket and a message came in from Reynolds. His free hand stroked her arms as he listened through the voicemail, then deleted it.

He tossed the phone on the bed, his mind flipping in disappointment. He reached back, pulling her around his body, cradling her in his lap. He kissed her before pulling back, his hands brushing through her hair.

"You're leaving, aren't you?"

"I'm sorry, baby, I have to go."

"What's going on?"

"Loose ends."

"What loose ends?"

He took a breath of hesitation about telling her the truth.

"Don't do it."

"We might have a lead on the locket," he said, pulling at her lips.

"And?"

He was unable to hide the smile that came with her stubborn nature, "Jorge Reynolds is asking to see me."

"Reynolds, as in Reynolds my stalker, psycho murderer, Reynolds?"

He kept her eyes and he nodded.

"Why does he want to see you?"

"I don't know, he won't say."

"What do you think he wants?"

"He could want to talk about you."

"Me, why, me?"

"Well he did help me find you and he told us about the locket."

"He did?" She sat up in his arms, her attention focused on the conversation.

"Yep."

"So, you think he wants to talk to you, to find out what happened?"

"Maybe, or he may just want to talk about you."

"What are you going to do?"

"I haven't decided yet." Eric lifted her with his arms and twisted, laying her back on the bed.

"What would make you want to go see him?"

"There are several things," he lay beside her and she rolled onto her side to face him. "I think he might be able to tell me who has the locket."

"So you're going to go see him."

"I didn't say that." He played with her hair, loving her sudden interrogation of him.

"You didn't not say it either, Stiles." She lined his chin before kissing him. "When you go see him, just promise me you'll be careful."

"If I—"

"Promise."

"It's a jail—"

"Promise, Stiles."

"I promise." He smirked, pulling her beneath him again before smothering her mouth.

"You see, that wasn't so difficult, was it?"

"Not nearly as difficult as it's going to be to leave you today." He kissed her once more before rising off the bed and heading to the bathroom. He took a quick shower and got dressed. He walked into the bedroom to see that she'd curled beneath the blankets and fallen back to sleep.

He crouched next to the bed and caressed her face. Her eyes opened to look at him.

"I love you," he said into her lips. He kissed her and she kissed him back with a sleepy smile.

"I love you, too," she said, caressing his cheek. "Be safe."

"I will. Go back to sleep." He kissed her again before rising to leave.

Eric closed the bedroom door as he left, hoping that she would sleep. He walked into the kitchen and took a breath of patience. Lucy was sitting on top of the island with a bowl of cereal.

He knew that Rebecca loved her sister. For that reason alone, he tolerated Lucy's temporary presence in the house. She was supposed to be going back to the rehab center to finish her therapy. At the last minute, she'd convinced Beccs that she was too scared to go back after the abduction. While it seemed like a plausible explanation, for whatever reason, he didn't buy it.

The conditions of her staying at the house were that she attended an outpatient program and got a job. So far, he saw no evidence of either. He didn't like the way she treated Beccs. His gut told him not to trust her and his gut was never wrong.

"Well, if it isn't the noble detective."

Eric walked past her into the kitchen

"Stop by for a booty call before your shift?"

"Funny. At least I have somewhere to go."

"I would, too, if I could leave Beccs home for half a second without her having a nervous breakdown."

He ignored her.

"No thanks to you, by the way."

"I can take care of Beccs just fine, Lucy," Eric kept his voice light and even. "So go, live your life. She'll be okay without you, I promise."

"I might be able to believe that if you were around a little more here, Stiles." She threw the comment back.

He gave up trying.

"Speaking of her highness, is Beccs up?"

"Not yet and please let her sleep." He took a water out of the fridge before grabbing his keys off the counter.

"So what, we'll see you in two, three days?"

"I'll be home tonight."

"Hope you didn't promise Beccs. You don't need to disappoint her again."

She thought of his early morning kisses, drifting in and out, hovering in comfortable warmth. A loud thumping erupted in her ears. She opened her eyes and realized it was the stereo in the living room.

It was just before eight. She pulled herself out of bed, yanking open the bedroom door. Hit by a wave of music, she winced and walked straight to the stereo, turning it off.

"Hey!"

Rebecca turned toward her voice, finding her in the kitchen.

"Oh I'm sorry, were you sleeping? Eric said you were up."

"It's fine." She scratched her neck in mild irritation and walked into the kitchen to start some coffee.

"So what are your plans today, Beccs?"

"I, uh," she started with a yawn. "I am going to get caught up on some work, maybe have lunch with Donna, why? Did you need something?"

"No, it's fine," she replied with a shrug. "I'll figure something out."

"Are you sure?" Rebecca poured water into the coffeemaker.

"Well, I have a job interview this afternoon," Lucy started. "It's at a real estate office. Well, you know how conservative those people are and I don't really have anything suitable to wear. I really want to get this job, Beccs. I want to start pulling my weight around here. You and Eric have been so great about everything."

"Okay." Rebecca walked to her purse, grabbing her wallet. "Here's my card, go get what you need."

"Really?"

"Sure." She smiled, seeing her sister's excitement. "You need a suit and I know you don't have one, so go get one."

"Oh, you're the best." Lucy pulled her into a hug. "I love you, Beccs."

"I love you, too, Lucy," she released her and stepped back. "I'm going to jump into the shower. Did you need me to take you to the mall?"

"No, I couldn't ask that, you already have your day planned," Lucy said." I can totally take the bus."

"You sure?"

"Of course!"

"Okay, good luck today.

Rebecca walked out of the bedroom an hour or so later refreshed and relaxed. She was ready to dig out from under the work mountain. She set herself up in the kitchen, pulled the stool over to the counter, ready for the onslaught. She picked up her coffee cup when she noticed two bags beside the door of Lucy's room. She walked to the door, looking inside the bags. Her heart suddenly spiked a chest-curling ache seeing the pile of baby clothes and toys filling the bags. She quickly took a step back before the crushing emotion could overwhelm her. She recovered with a deep breath and saw a note attached to the bag.

Beccs,
I realized that these need to go back today. Can you please take

them back to the store? The receipt's in the bag.

Love you, Lucy

Rebecca crumpled the note in her hand and grabbed the bags off the floor. She retrieved her purse off the counter, locked the house and headed out.

Chapter Eight

He sat down and loaded the file he'd received from the warden. In his quest to locate the locket, he'd thought about his conversation with Rebecca and remembered Reynolds' demand to see him just before her abduction. The warden of the prison reported he'd had a visitor just before she disappeared. In curiosity, Eric requested the surveillance. He watched the file and saw the visitor come into view. His stomach dropped. Her face was hidden behind a large pair of sunglasses, besides that, she was a dead ringer for Rebecca. He looked for any indication as to who the woman was, but there was nothing, just the name Abigail Lockhart.

He switched over to the video feed from the parking lot. He watched a car pull up and the woman stepped out. He couldn't get a good view of the driver. The woman disappeared from the frame and the car moved. The sun passed over the car, illuminating the man's face.

"Eric, Carl's ready for us."

"I'll be right there," Eric said as he clipped the image, attached it to an email and sent it off for identification.

"Stiles."

"What's up?" Eric stood beside Lug, popped four Advil in his mouth and swallowed.

"We picked up some buzz on the locket."

"What kind of buzz?"

"The kind that says that it's up for sale again."

"So soon? Are they stupid?"

"I guess the potato is too hot to hold."

"Any specifics?"

"Not yet."

"Adam and I were going to go talk to Carl, you want to join?"

"Yeah, let's go." They walked into the tech unit. Adam was waiting for them and Eric smiled when he saw Carl working on their mysterious black box.

"Stiles and in one piece no less," Carl extended his hand.

Eric shook it. "Wouldn't be here without you, man."

"Damn straight. So I'm assuming you're here about our box."

"Yeah, what have you got for us?"

"Actually your timing is perfect. I just broke through the perimeter."

"What does that mean?" Lug looked to Adam in confusion.

"He got through whatever defenses were built into the box to hide its secrets."

"Okay, I'm with you."

"So what did you find?"

"Well, I can tell you what it looks like," Carl's focus was on his computer monitor. "At first glance it is a decryption device."

"You mean like in codes?"

"Yeah."

"So the chip is encrypted. According to the interviews, Gregorn was going to need this box to get to the files?"

"Yeah. Do you have any idea what was on the chip?"

"Uh . . . no, not unless Gregorn told us in his interview."

"He didn't, I checked," Carl shook his head with a sigh. "Okay look, unless our cartel has some serious government connections, that chip is way out of their league."

"So the information doesn't match the security," Eric

surmised, looking to Lug and Adam.

"Hell no, this is like sticking cubic zirconium in Fort Knox. You have to understand, if this is the only thing that can decrypt the codes," Carl explained, "which I am going to assume is the case. Considering just how hard it is to get your hands on one of these, that chip is not protecting anything connected to a drug cartel. This thing is meant for international secrets, which means you guys have a serious problem."

Rebecca stood at the counter, trying not to look around the exclusive baby super mart. It was hard enough walking in the doors, much less looking around at the array of heartbreakingly adorable baby items.

"What's the reason for return?"

Rebecca found herself at a loss." Not needed."

"I'm sorry, I hate to ask that question," the girl commented, looking uncomfortably. "It's so insensitive."

"It's okay," Rebecca responded with an understanding nod. She pushed away the heavy feeling in her chest.

"I'll need to see your card to do the refund, ma'am." Rebecca looked up in surprise.

"Oh, I'm sorry. I thought it was a cash sale," she started in confusion. "I . . . uh don't have the card with me."

"That's not a problem, we can just do a store credit," the clerk replied with a smile.

Rebecca's mind continued to buzz.

"Unless you want to come back another time?"

"No, a store credit is fine, thanks."

Lucy got a new card . . . that's odd.

"Is there any way you could make a copy of the original receipt for me?"

"Not a problem," the clerk turned away from the counter.

Rebecca's phone rang in her purse. "This is Rebecca."

"Is this Rebecca Gailen?"

"Yes, may I ask who is calling?"

"Hello, Ms. Gailen, my name is Kathy and I am with Chase International. I'm sorry to bother you, but a fraud alert came up on your card this afternoon."

"What kind of alert?"

"We have recorded a purchase of two planes tickets through a third-party internet site. Was this an authorized purchase, Ms. Gailen?"

"No, it wasn't, I didn't . . ." she realized the card they were talking about was the same card she gave Lucy that morning. "I didn't authorize the purchase, but I need to check with someone. What happens now?"

"We would put a suspension on your card," Kathy replied. "To prevent any additional unauthorized purchases."

"Instead of suspending, can you put a monitor on the account for the next twenty-four hours?"

"Will you take responsibility for any purchases made to the card?"

"Yes, I will," she agreed, her mind racing. "Can you email me a list of all of the purchases at the end of business today?"

"Sure, what is your email address?"

"Send it to rgailen at live dot com."

"Not a problem," Kathy replied. "Would you like us to contact the police, Ms. Gailen?"

"No, I will be doing that myself. Thank you though."

"Would you mind if I followed up with you tomorrow on the status of the account, ma'am?"

"Not at all. Please call me at this number anytime," Rebecca pushed her hand through her hair and ended the call.

"Here you are, ma'am," the clerk handed Rebecca the receipt.

"Thank you." She threw the receipt in her bag, distracted

by the phone call. Rebecca called Eric and got his voicemail. Hanging up the phone, she typed him a text message, her phone ringing in the same moment.

"This is Rebecca."

"Beccs, hey, I'm sorry, sweetie, but I am going to have to cancel our lunch."

"Oh that's okay, Don, don't worry about it."

"Are you sure?"

"Yeah, it's fine. I have stuff I need to catch up on anyway."

"I'll stop by after work, okay?"

"Yeah, that would be great. I'll see you then."

The call from the credit card company nagged at her. She wondered what Lucy would need with plane tickets. She wanted to talk to Eric before she did anything, but he still wasn't answering his phone.

She dropped her purse on the counter as she walked into the house, seeing the receipt from the baby store fall onto the floor. She grabbed it off the floor and began sorting through her emails as her conversation with the credit card company reran in her mind.

Her hand brushed against the receipt and something clicked.

"The minimum balance due is three thousand eight hundred and fifty dollars," the man quoted over the phone.

"That is the minimum payment?"

"Yes, Ms. Gailen."

"Can you tell me what the full balance is?"

"As of today, the balance stands at thirty-three thousand five hundred and sixty dollars."

She resorted her email and then saw it. The gentleman

from a few weeks before had sent her a copy of the bill just requested. She opened the attachment and looked down the purchases. She double checked the account number and realized it was the card she'd co-signed with Lucy for school.

Her heart began pounding and she fought to breathe.

She picked up the baby store receipt.

It has to be a mistake . . .

Her heart was still pounding when she walked into the station. Her mind a twisted, gapping mess of pain as she searched for him. She walked in and said hello to the desk sergeant. "Is Detective Stiles here?"

"Hello, Ms. Gailen, he should be at his desk."

"Do you mind if I go back? I really need to speak with him."

"Sure thing, just sign in and go ahead back."

"Thanks."

She took the elevator up and made her way through the office until she reached his desk. He and Adam were both missing and she felt her chest filling with panic.

"Rebecca?"

She jumped five feet as she turned.

"Whoa."

"Lug . . ."

"Sorry I didn't mean to scare you," he said, looking at her in concern.

"Are you looking for Eric? What's wrong?"

"Yeah . . . I . . . uh . . ." She looked down at the paper in her hands. "Lug, I need your help."

"Sure, anything," he said with a reassuring nod. "Let's go in here so we can talk." He ushered her into a conference room and closed the door behind them. "What's up?"

"I . . ."

"Just start at the beginning."

She nodded and relayed the story about the credit cards. She handed him the statements as she finished. "The receipt from the baby . . . from the store is on the bottom."

Lugow read over the documents and looked up at her with a sigh.

"Tell me I am overreacting. That I'm reading too much into this."

"Rebecca, I—" he was interrupted by his phone." This is Detective Lugow. Hey . . . ah yeah . . . conference room A6. Yeah . . . okay."

"Was that Eric?"

"Yeah, he's on his way."

"I'm not overreacting, am I?"

"I don't think so. I'm sorry, Rebecca."

"You're kidding me," Eric took a step back in shock.

"I wish I was. You should see the paperwork that came when I brought this guy up. Red flags everywhere. I am not sure what he did, but there is definitely a reason he is not working for the DEA anymore."

"You're sure?"

"Positive," AJ, their facial analyst, nodded as he printed something. "You said you got this from the prison security feed?"

"Yeah."

"Interesting."

"What, why?"

"Usually, the prisons have facial recognition built into the security protocols. I wonder why this guy didn't pop up."

"Thanks, AJ."

"Anytime," the man replied as Eric walked across the hall, heading to the vending machine. He pulled out some quarters and popped a soda, mulling the new development.

So a mystery girl, looking like Rebecca, shows up to talk to Reynolds with an ex-DEA agent? On top of the locket, it sounded like they needed to make a trip.

"Hey, Stiles, did your girlfind you?"

"What?"

"Your girl, Becky, she's here," Jerry, the desk sergeant, replied as he continued down the hall.

Eric made a beeline for his desk and saw no one. He scanned the area and picked up the phone, dialing Lug. Perhaps when he wasn't here, she went down to see him. "Lug, hey, is Rebecca with you?"

"Hey, yeah."

"Where are you?"

"Conference room A6"

"Is she okay?"

"Yeah."

"I'll be right there."

Adam walked to his desk. "Where are you going?"

"Uh . . . Rebecca's here. Lug has her in a conference room." Eric walked a few feet down the hall.

"What's going on?"

"I don't know," Eric scanned his badge and opened the door. He saw her in the corner of the room, her arms folded over her chest. "Beccs, what's going on?"

"Rebecca brought you, well . . . us some information."

Eric turned to Lug, standing a few feet away." What information?"

"You'd better sit down."

Eric looked to Rebecca and then to Lug. He took a seat and Lug explained the situation. At the end of it, Eric scratched the back of his neck in apprehension.

"What do you think?"

"I think it makes sense."

"What do you mean, why?" Rebecca looked to him in

interest.

"It just does." Eric held back the details of what happened at the prison. Unfortunately, as soon as he said it, he realized she could see right through him. He met her eyes and she scolded him for holding back again. "A woman came to see Reynolds a few weeks ago. She was a dead ringer for you, signed in as Abigail Lockhart."

Her face drained of color and Rebecca grabbed for the chair for support.

"Beccs..." Eric moved to her side, his arm wrapping around her in support.

"You said Abigail Lockhart?" she asked and he nodded looking at her in confusion. "That's my mother's name... her maiden name."

Eric looked to Adam and Lugow.

"Do we have any idea about what happened or what they talked about?" Adam asked.

"Not yet."

"We have to talk to Reynolds," she said, her eyes dark and apprehensive.

"Rebecca..." Lug and Adam both started to object.

"It's the only way we are going to know for sure."

"Beccs..."

"Eric, I have to know if she did this. I have to know if Lucy was the one who..." The emotion in her eyes called to him in desperation. "If she was, then she probably planned this whole thing and she has the locket. According to this, she is going to disappear tomorrow night with it if we don't do something!"

"There is no we in the scenario, Rebecca."

"The hell there isn't!"

"Stiles, she's got a point."

"It's not happening..."

Adam quickly interjected. "We understand your concern,

but all of this is moot until we can verify that she in fact has instigated this whole scenario."

"Which means, if she does have the locket and they are planning to use the tickets, we are out of time," Lug said.

"There is only one person who can tell us that," Adam added.

Eric lost his cool and moved to the door. He walked out of the conference room, closing the door behind him. All he could see was red. The thought of allowing . . .

"*Eric!*"

He stopped to face her.

"Rebecca, I'm not doing this with you."

"You're right, because I'm coming with you."

"No, you're not."

"You'll have a better chance if I go with you."

Eric grabbed her hand and pulled her into an empty office. He closed the door and shut the blinds. "I don't care."

"Eric—"

"No."

"Why?"

"You don't need to be feeding into his fantasy." He saw the fire of determination in her eyes. He knew the argument was pointless and yet he continued. "Even if he wasn't the instigator, he's still psychotic, Rebecca, and he's fixated on you."

"And he's behind bars. He can't hurt me. You made sure of that!"

"Beccs—" he turned away from her.

"I can do this. We can do this, Eric."

"No. You're in no condition . . ."

"Screw you, I'm not a child!"

"Beccs—"

"No!" Her eyes glared at him." I don't need your permission to do this! Adam and Lug will take me down there right now and I will do this alone if I have to!"

"That's not—"

"I know you are trying to protect me and I love you for that." Her eyes pleaded with him. "But I need to do this. I need to know the truth."

"Sweetheart, it's not worth it."

"Yes, it is. It is to me. I have to know if she did this to me . . . to us." She stepped up to his chest, lacing her fingers through his. "Please don't make me do this without you. I need you to understand that I have to do this, Eric."

He took a deep breath, knowing that he didn't have a choice. She was going to go with or without him. Looking down into her pleading but determined eyes, his resolve melted. He wrapped his hands in her hair as he moved to her, pulling her to his lips. He kissed her before he pulled back. "Fine, we'll go see him together, but we're doing this my way. No arguments."

"No arguments, I promise."

He didn't like this.

His entire body rejected the notion of allowing her in the same room with that monster. He still couldn't believe she'd talked him into it.

If Lucy had instigated the stalking and now had the locket, she was right. It was their best option to getting the truth. They decided that she would speak to him alone. If Reynolds got out of control or started playing games, Eric and Lugow would step in. His stomach continued to flip as he glanced at Lug. Eric knew he could count on him to back him up and make sure things stayed within their control.

Reynolds was waiting. His hands and feet shackled to the chair and table. The door opened and Rebecca stepped into the room. Eric and Lug watched from the observation area.

"Rebecca, it's so good to see you," Reynolds said with

what could only be described as a purr. "I'd dreamt of it several times, but I never expected to see you so soon. I knew you couldn't stay away."

"I need to ask you a question." Her voice even and her eyes steady, masking any fear she may have had.

"Delightful."

"Do you know my sister?"

"Intriguing," Reynolds replied with a wide smile. "He told you, didn't he?"

"Who told me?

"Detective Stiles."

"What was he supposed to tell me?"

"I'll answer all of your questions. However, you have to play by the rules just like your white knight."

"I don't understand."

"I'll answer your question, if you answer mine."

"Fine."

"Yummy, I'll go first," he replied as he licked his lips.

A chill crawled up Eric's spine as he looked to Lug in hesitation.

"Do you still dream about me, Rebecca? I'll know if you're lying."

"Yes," she replied with no hint of emotion.

Eric watched him studying her.

"My turn. Do you know my sister?"

"Little Lucy? Yes, I know Lucy very well."

"Did she . . ."

"Ah, not yet," he said, ticking his finger at her in amusement. "Do you feel safe in his arms?"

"Yes. Did my sister ask you to stalk me?"

"Oh, my lovely sunshine. The sparkle has died from your eyes, Beccs."

"Don't call me that."

"I'm curious. Did it fade away before or after your baby

died?"

"Answer my question."

"I have a feeling it started to extinguish just before. The painful loss of your child finally doused the fire that lit you from within."

"Answer the question."

"It is rather disappointing, I must say. To lose the enthralling fire that drew me in. I can only imagine the effect it's having on Eric."

"Stop it."

"I wonder how long it will take for him to drift away."

"You're not playing by the rules, Jorge. Tell me what I want to know."

"Can you feel him slipping away, Beccs?"

"Don't call me that. Answer my question."

"Did your prince tell you that we talked while you were gone?"

"I don't care what you did while I was gone. All I want is for you to answer my question!"

"His eyes were so helpless when you were—"

"Did she tell you to do it, Jorge?"

"You could see the emptiness in his eyes. Not unlike the cold hollow that has settled in yours, my love—"

"You don't know me."

"Oh, but I do."

"Was it my sister? Did she do this?"

"Your eyes tell me everything I need to know, they always have—"

"Answer the question, you superfluous bastard!" Rebecca slammed her fist on the table. His hand clenched around her wrist as he licked his lips.

"There's the fire. I can feel the heat pouring through you."

Eric moved as soon as Reynolds's hand reached for her. The door opened. Lug was quick to grab Reynolds by the shoulders. He yanked him back into the chair, forcing him to release her arm. Eric pulled her away from the table, using himself as a barrier between her and Reynolds.

"Like vanilla silk," Reynolds said to Eric, smelling the hand that was just wrapped around her wrist, his entire body visibly convulsing in delight. His eyes, focused on Rebecca, shone with unmistakable lust.

"Enough," Eric blocked Reynolds view of Rebecca. "Answer the question."

"Yes," Reynolds said, stretching his arms across the table.

"Why?" Rebecca's voice sounded small and breathless.

"That's not how the game's played, my love. You know the rules."

"No."

"Eric."

"No, we're done playing games with this asshole," Eric looked to Lug. "No banter, no psychological bullshit and no more playing puppet master. You're going to answer our questions or suffer the consequences."

"So aggressive, Detective Stiles, is this really necessary?" Reynolds challenged in disapproval, giving Eric a predatory gaze.

For the first time, Eric saw the darkness in the man, the psychosis that drove him. Eric leaned forward, getting inches away from the man's face." No, what's necessary is you disappearing into a deep, dark hole. Where the only thing you'll have to play with is the fading memory of your life before you touched her. Answer the question."

"Because you are her sister, Rebecca." Reynolds laughed. "Who else is she going to blame for her problems? Your rotting mother?"

"What about the locket?" she said, her voice shaking. "Does she have the locket?"

"Ah, the locket," he sat back in his chair with a knowing

smile before his eyes closed." Your lips are so much more luscious in person. I can hear your breath escaping through them in a wanting moan."

"Tell us what you know." Lug gripped Reynolds' shoulders in warning.

"Of course she has the locket. That's been her drive all along. She used it as an excuse to torture you, Rebecca. Knowing that it would keep everyone occupied for a while. I, of course, was more than happy to oblige."

"Where did she get the chip?"

"No idea, she wasn't exactly a plethora of information like you. Tell me, Beccs," Reynolds looked at her with interest in his eyes." Does it make it better or worse knowing that my affections while I assure you are genuine were forced by another?"

"Did Marco know what Lucy was doing? Is that why—"

"Oh, please, Lucy doesn't know what she's doing half the time and they say I'm crazy." Reynolds shook his head. "No, he was a puppet just like the rest of us. When she told me he was on his way, I knew things were about to come to a head. You see, she needed Marco to get the locket back. She couldn't break herself out of rehab, now could she? I am just so sorry I missed it. It is really a shame that my brother went and got himself killed. I would've liked to have heard the details of his . . . time with you, Beccs."

"What's on the chip?"

"I've been more than cooperative," his eyes shifted briefly to Eric before licking his lips as his gaze ran up and down Rebecca's body. "Now, I expect something in return."

"It's not going to happen."

Reynolds sniffed the palm of his hand once again.

Eric felt Rebecca's body lurch and tremble against him. He pulled her closer to him.

"Have you watched her sleep, Detective?"

"We're done here." Eric banged on the door, keeping Rebecca at his side.

"The way her skin shines in the moonlight. The subtle rise and fall of her body as it breathes, her splendor," Reynolds said, his voice layered in envy.

Eric felt her trembles intensify as she gripped his arm.

"And you close your eyes, imagining her writhing lust-filled softness beneath you."

The door opened and Eric ushered her out of the room. He kept his hand on the small of her back as they walked down the hall and into the waiting area. The clang of the door echoed in the room and before he could say anything, she turned, burying herself in his chest.

Eric hugged her against him. He kissed the top of her head and held her until the door opened again and she shifted in his arms. Lug joined them and she raised herself off his chest, looking at their friend with a steady gaze.

"So, what happens now?"

"Now we find Lucy."

Chapter Nine

*Who else is she going to blame for her problems?
Your rotting mother?*

"Are you okay to drive?"

"Yeah, I'm fine," Rebecca pulled herself out of her head and unlocked the car. "I'll meet you at the house."

"Beccs."

She felt Eric's hand in her hair as she faced him.

"We're going to figure this out."

She stared into his clear blue eyes and her body calmed. He leaned over, brushing a tender kiss over her lips before releasing her with a smile. She turned and got into her car. He waited until she closed the door before crossing the parking lot to his truck.

Starting her car, she did her best to keep a clear head as she pulled out of the parking lot and headed home.

She didn't know what to think, feel or do. She drove in silence, reminded herself that she wasn't going to fall to pieces. She inhaled a deep breath and pushed back the anguish. Uncontrolled, her mind slipped back through all the clutter she'd been suppressing. As if she'd popped a balloon, all the air left her lungs.

Images, threats and fear coursed through her body as all the horrid memories crashed over her again. Her still-tender wounds were ripped open. The knowledge that it was her own sister who had invoked them tore her insides apart.

Unable to bite back the wave of nausea that began to erupt in her stomach, she pulled off the road. She thrust the door open and ran away from the car before unleashing the contents of her stomach behind a desert bush.

Rebecca cursed her body, hearing Eric's truck door close behind her. Her stomach clenched again and she heaved forward, unable to stop the ripple of bile. His hands in her hair, she wiped her mouth before she straightened her back and found herself facing him.

"Are you okay?"

She nodded wordlessly before taking a deep breath." I'm good." Her eyes watered in frustration. "I must've eaten something bad."

"Beccs," he looked at her, concern in his eyes.

"Eric, I'm fine," she turned out of his arms and moved back to the car. "We need to get going."

"Hey," he reached out, catching her wrist. "Beccs, wait."

"We need to go—"

"It can wait a few minutes." He pulled her toward him.

She struggled to keep her emotions restrained.

"Rebecca, look at me."

"Eric . . ." she automatically resisted, knowing that as soon as she did, there was no coming back. "I can't."

"You can't what, look at me? Don't shut me out, Beccs."

"I'm not!"

"Yes, you are! You accused me of censoring our conversations this morning, but you're doing the same thing!"

"No, I'm not—"

"Then tell me what you're thinking."

"I'm thinking that we're wasting time!"

"No." Before she could turn away, he tangled his fingers in her hair, framing her face. "You're reliving every moment. Every threat, every scream and every chill because now it isn't some random asshole. It's your sister. That's why you stopped the car."

Her stomach dropped and she lost her breath, startled by

his words. She lowered her eyes, fighting the bubbling tears that threatened to pour out.

"I know you, sweetheart. I can see it in your eyes. You think you're hiding it from me, but you're not." He leaned down to catch her eyes again. "When are you going to figure out that you don't have to be strong for me?"

"I don't need you to hold me up, Eric."

"I know you don't, but you don't have to be a wall of steel either."

"I . . . I just don't want to be one of those pathetic women who can't handle anything. I feel like I'm not being fair to you."

"Rebecca, you're the strongest person I know." His forehead touched hers as he wrapped his arms around her waist.

As soon as he did, her entire body relaxed. She loved that he could ease her mind and body with a look, but it made it difficult to keep her armor intact.

"With everything that's happened, you're allowed to fall apart once in a while. In fact, you had me almost frantic because you weren't reacting to what's happened."

"I should be able to handle it." She was still unable to admit he was tearing down her walls.

"Okay fine, if you have to be this wall of steel, you're allowed to with everyone else. Not me, Beccs, not me."

She looked at him in irritation.

"I promised not to censor our conversations this morning. Now, I want you to do the same. I want you to be honest with me and stop acting like you are unaffected."

She struggled with letting him back in and after everything, it shouldn't be a concern. However, she felt like she shouldn't dump everything on him. His clear eyes stared down her and she could see that he wanted her to lean on him. He wanted to know when she was struggling or hurting.

She contemplated it, putting herself in his shoes. If he was holding back his struggles, his fears, she would be frustrated and worried about him. She would want him to talk to her and lean on her. Why was it so difficult to allow herself to do just that?

You can trust him Beccs. He's not like the others.

Rebecca nodded in agreement, seeing him smile and her eyes filled with tears. Her arms around his neck, she clung to him. Her body released all the tension and pain she'd built up since they left the hospital.

"That's my girl." Eric held her tightly against him.

She felt safe. "I refuse to be a weeping, weak, idiot, outside of right here," she defined, lowering herself back down, her hand resting on his chest.

"I think I can handle that." He kissed her forehead.

"And if I get to be too needy, I expect you to tell me, Stiles."

"I don't think it'll be a problem."

"You say that now, but you may not feel that way after a while—"

"Yes, I will."

"Oh really?"

"I kinda like you needing me." He leaned down, tugging at her lips.

"So, this was your plan all along. You're just trying to keep me helplessly attached to you."

"Guilty as charged." Eric smirked before capturing her lips in a tender kiss.

"I love you, Stiles."

"I love you, too."

"Eric," her gaze trailed down to his shirt. "What are we going to do?"

"I don't know, baby," Eric pulled her closer.

She let his warmth crash over her, soothing her anguished mind.

"We'll figure it out."

Ten minutes from the house, she wanted a hot bath and a nap. The chances of that happening were close to impossible. They had to figure out what to do about Lucy and she knew Eric was already on the phone with Adam.

Her phone rang and she reached into her purse, pulling it out. Not recognizing the number, she contemplated whether she was going to answer. "This is Rebecca."

"Beccs, where are you?" Lucy asked.

Her stomach dropped. "I'm, uh... I'm driving home. What's up, sweetie?" Rebecca gulped back the emotion in her voice.

"I got the job!"

"You did, that's great," she tried to sound as enthusiastic as possible, her gaze darting back to Eric's truck. "We should celebrate!"

"Really?"

"Of course," her mind raced as her heart thudded in her chest. "I'll call Charlie and we can have a party at the bar."

"At the Rustic?"

"Yeah, there's no better place and where else can we get free drinks?"

"Can I invite some friends?"

"Of course," she still wondered if she was doing the right thing. "Why don't you meet me at the house? We'll make all the arrangements and then we can get ready together."

"Uh, okay, but I have to do a ton of paperwork before I leave here. You know, new hire stuff. So, I'll meet you in a few hours?"

"Perfect, I'll call Charlie right now."

"What about Eric, you're going to call him, aren't you?"

"Yeah, of course, but I don't think he'll be able to come. He's been really busy."

"Beccs, I know you love him and all, but you really deserve better."

"Yeah." The comment stabbed, reinforcing her sister's betrayal. Rebecca held back the wetness in her eyes. "Maybe we can talk about it when you get home."

"Deal, I'll see you in a few hours."

"Bye," Rebecca replied, hung up the phone and turned into her driveway. She collected herself and headed to the door, feeling Eric just behind her. He entered the alarm code and she dropped her purse on the couch. Desperate to remain in control, she pushed her fingers through her hair.

"I was thinking on the way here—"

"She called me."

"What?"

"Lucy, she called me on my cell on the way here."

He moved closer.

She found strength in his gentle eyes.

"What happened?"

"She was calling to tell me she got the job," she took a deep breath, determined not to crumble. "She sounded excited about it and so I did the only thing I could think of. I suggested that we celebrate."

"Celebrate?"

"I told her I would call Charlie and we could have a celebration party at the bar." Rebecca looked for some sign that she'd done the right thing. "I suggested that she come home and we could get ready together."

"And she agreed?"

"It took a little convincing, but she'll be here in a few hours." She could see his mind racing and he looked away from her in distraction. "Eric . . ."

"I'm going to call Donna and I want you—"

"No."

"What?"

"I'm not leaving."

"Baby, you can't stay."

"I have to stay," she met his gaze. "She's not going to just give it to you. She doesn't trust you as it is."

"It's not your problem. I'll figure something out."

"It's not going to work,"

He turned in frustration.

"I know my sister, Eric. As soon as she realizes what is happening, she's going to clam up. Any chance we have of getting the locket back is going to disappear."

"I won't ask you to do this." Concern and hesitation shone in his eyes.

"I need to do this." She was desperate to keep the tremor out of her voice.

"Just like you needed to see Reynolds?"

"Yes."

"And that went so well!"

"We got what we needed, didn't we?"

"But at what price, Beccs? You can only take so much. You don't need to—"

"It's all a part of the same thing," she replied, looking up into his loving eyes. "Don't you see? If I don't, it's never going to end."

It took them forty-five minutes to wire the house and set up the truck down the street. They decided not to wire Rebecca, concerned about her getting caught. Instead, they opted for a simple earpiece so Eric could stay in constant communication if she needed him. Everything was set and now all they could do was wait.

The plan was for Rebecca to gain Lucy's trust and get her to talk about the locket. Once that happened, step two was to get her to reveal where it was and then what she was planning to do with it.

Eric waited in the truck with Adam and Lug. The operation was low risk, but he still had his concerns. Specifically, in regards to Rebecca's need for closure. He understood it and supported it. However, he also knew that she was more vulnerable than she let on. So he kept reminding himself that she is his tough-as-nails, fiery redhead. After this was all over, he would be the one to hold her as it all fell away.

"You think she can pull this off?"

"I know she can." Eric realized that he wasn't concerned about what happened right now. It was after that worried him.

"So why do you look like you're going to jump out of your skin?"

"Just want it to be over."

"Looks like you're going to get your wish," Adam said.

Eric's attention turned to the monitor.

"Here we go."

"Beccs, Lucy just pulled up. You ready?"

"Yeah. I'm good."

"I'm right here if you need me."

"Eric, she's not alone," Adam warned.

"Who's with her?"

"A guy. I'm trying to get a shot of his face." Lug worked on the computer.

Eric's focus returned to the monitor.

Lucy walked in the door, followed by a large, burly man.

"Hey, sweetie," Rebecca moved across the room toward her sister. "Who's your friend?"

"Beccs, this is Doug. Doug, this is my sister Rebecca."

Rebecca reached out, taking Doug's hand.

Eric was able to get a good look at his face. Something nagged at him. He knew him, but didn't know from where.

"Nice to meet you, Doug."

"Doug can you hang out here for a while? My sister and I need to have some girl talk," Lucy giggled before she grabbed Rebecca's hand, leading her into the guestroom.

"Where did you meet him?"

"At the real estate office. He was looking at houses with one of the reps," Lucy pulled off her shirt and began to change. "He's totally hot, right?"

"I'm not arguing. So tell me about the job."

"Well I start on Tuesday and it's from seven to noon three days a week. But they said if I do a good job and I'm reliable, that they'll increase my hours."

"That's great, Lucy!"

"And the best part is that after my three-month probation, I can attend the real estate classes for free."

"Is that something you'd be interested in?"

"I dunno, maybe. It's a start, right?"

"That it is,"

Eric watched her hand go through her hair and he knew she was struggling.

"Hey, you never showed me the suit you got today. Did it help you get the job?"

"Definitely."

"So where is it?"

"Oh, well I have a confession."

"What?"

"Well, I wore the suit, but I left the tags on and then took it back."

"Why on earth would you do that?"

"It was expensive and I felt bad spending your money, sis."

"Lucy, it's fine. I wanted you to get something for yourself," Rebecca reached out, taking her sister's hands as they sat on the bed together. "You didn't have to do that."

"Damn it!" Eric swore as the face of the man hit him.
"What's wrong?"
"It's him."
"Who?"
"He's the same guy from the prison. He's ex-DEA." His heart leapt, knowing the situation had become dangerous. "I also saw him at the Rehab center with Lucy. She's been working with him the whole time! Call AJ, see what we know about him."

How the hell am I going to do this?
She needed to find the locket, but she'd no idea where to start. They'd already searched her room and found nothing. Which meant she had it on her, hidden somewhere, or it was gone.
Okay, Beccs, think . . . you can do this.
"I'm going to jump in the shower." Rebecca realized she'd tuned her sister out. "Hey, Lucy, I was thinking," Rebecca prayed that she was doing the right thing. "Instead of going to Charlie's tonight, how about a girl's night out. Just you and me?"
"Are you serious?"
"Of course," Rebecca gave her sister a wide smile. "It's been forever since we've spent any time together. I could definitely use some fun. So what do you think?" Rebecca watched Lucy as she studied her before she nodded in agreement.
"I'd love to," she said with a matched grin. "I guess I need to get rid of Doug for a while, huh?"
"Unless you want him to come along. Although, I think he might take away from the fun . . ."
"Yeah, he does tend to overreact," she said with a giggle.

"I'll go talk to him."

"And I'll get ready." Lucy walked into the living room and Rebecca shut the door of her bedroom. She tried to listen to the conversation when she heard Eric's voice.

"Rebecca, what are you doing?" His voice was thick with frustration and she took a breath before answering him. "Beccs . . ."

"I need you to trust me." She walked into her closet. "I know what I'm doing, Eric."

"Can you at least tell me what you're going to do?"

"Girl's night out." She searched her closet for a suitable outfit. "We're going to start at The Beach and wind up at The Rustic."

"I don't like this."

"Well, it's all I've got. Unless you're planning to come in here and arrest her now, we need to make it work." She chose a revealing shirt and her leather mini. "Set it up and I'll meet you at the Rustic at one thirty."

"I'm going with you."

Her heart skipped, and her mind envisioned the night ahead of her. "No."

"Beccs, you're not going to do this alone."

"You're right," Rebecca pulled out her patent leather boots. "That's why Lugow is coming with me."

"Bec—"

"Lucy doesn't know him. He can stay in plain sight and close. Have him meet me at The Beach in an hour. I need to get changed before she gets suspicious. So could you please ask Lug to turn off the monitors for a couple of minutes?"

"Beccs, are you sure about this?"

"I love you, Eric."

"I love you, too."

Rebecca changed into what Mindy had called her man-killer outfit. She did her makeup and hair. Half an hour later, she heard the door of her bedroom open.

Lucy's head popped into the room. "Are you . . ." she smiled as she saw what her sister was wearing. "Damn, Beccs, I didn't think you had it in you."

"I told you we were going out for some fun." Rebecca laughed. She checked her hair once more before walking out of the bathroom. "Are you ready to hit the road?"

"Definitely, where are we going?"

"You'll see."

"She's got a point," Lug looked to Eric as if negotiating. "I can get closer than you can."

"You're not helping."

"You're the one who said she could do this, Stiles," Lug said. "I know that this whole thing is a mess and complicated, but you need to let her do it. I promise I'll watch out for her and she'll be fine."

"I know. I just have this feeling that she doesn't want me there."

"She doesn't."

Eric turned looking to Adam.

"Come on, Stiles, if you needed to go undercover to obtain specific information, would you really want Rebecca watching?"

"So not helping."

"Look, do you trust her?" Lug interjected.

"Of course."

"Then trust her."

Eric heard what they were was saying, but that didn't mean he had to like it. To keep the burning in his stomach under control, he reminded himself that when it was over, he'd be the one holding her and maybe finally they could move on.

Chapter Ten

She tried to block out the repeated chanting, telling herself to relax. She would normally think of Eric to relax, but in this case, it would make things so much worse.

"Shot, Shot, Shot, Shot . . ."

She forced herself to smile as she tilted her head back and opened her mouth. The stream of alcohol filled her cheeks and she turned to her nameless partner, a dirty grin covering his face as she fed him the shot via her mouth. She tried to remain reserved, but the man's tongue snaked itself into her mouth. The crowd cheered and she pulled away.

He proceeded to stand and raise his arms in conquest.

Someone handed Rebecca a towel and she wiped herself off. With the assistance of two bartenders, she got off the top of the bar and received cheers of her own.

"Who are you and what have you done with my sister?"

"Did you really think I was that much of a prude, Lucy?"

"Yes."

"Wow, I'm insulted."

"Well, Beccs, you're dating a cop."

"What does that have to do with anything?"

"Oh come on! Stiles is as righteous as they come!"

"No, he's not. You just haven't seen his dark side, trust me."

"Oh okay . . . yeah right." They received two shots and clinked their glasses together before downing them. "You want to dance?"

"Sure."

The music was heavy and Rebecca was vigilant to keep up with her sister's every move. Lucy was raising her arms high above her head and back against someone's chest when Rebecca saw a hint of gold.

Her gaze on her sister, she debated and then decided to take the chance. She danced up beside Lucy, positioning her current attachment against her sister while the music pounded and swirled. He was interested in what he saw and Rebecca pushed up behind him. She slid her hands down his arms before guiding them to her sister's abdomen. He seemed to be following her lead and he began to grind against her sister as his hands lifted her shirt to reveal her abdomen.

Lucy was lost in the music. She raised her arms to link around the neck of the man behind her and Rebecca saw it, plain as day.

The locket.

She must've been holding her breath because her vision began to sway. Rebecca couldn't get off the dance floor fast enough. The temperature dropped five degrees by just stepping off the platform and she took a breath. She felt someone behind her. She straightened her back before turning, ready to strike.

"Whoa."

Large hands wrapped around her wrists. "Lug—"

"Are you okay, your face is looking a little flushed?"

"Yeah, it's just a little hot out there."

"I can see why you didn't want Eric to come."

"Lug, I—" A wave of crushing guilt ripped through her and her heart pounded.

"It's cool. You're doing what you need to. I can see that it's not voluntary."

His eyes kept hers and she allowed herself to gulp in a long breath. "I found it."

"What?"

"The locket."

"Where?"

"She has it wrapped around her waist as a belly necklace."

"You're sure?"

"Positive."

"What's the plan, Ace?"

"Time for you to turn on the charm, Lugow."

His expression scrunched in discomfort.

"She is pretty buzzed. Let me get some more alcohol in her and she'll fall into your arms."

"You've been pounding them back just as hard. You—"

"I told the bartender that I'm an alcoholic. He's been giving me virgins all night."

"Nicely played, Beccs . . . I'm going to have to remember that one."

"Here she comes. I'll get some shots in her and then take her back onto the dance floor. That will be your cue." She walked away and he nodded in agreement. Rebecca took a seat at the bar. With a wink and a twenty, she ordered two rounds of shots. Within minutes, Lucy joined her.

"Where did you go?" She took a seat, breathless.

"Bathroom break, sorry."

"Why didn't you tell me? I got practically mauled out there without you!"

"Oh please, you loved it."

The bartender arrived with their shots.

"Okay I did. Ggod I'm so hot . . .'"

"Shots."

"Shots!" They took down the first set.

Lucy looked to her with a lopsided grin. "I have to admit, Beccs, I thought this was going to suck! You've been such a drag lately."

"I'm glad you're having a good time."

"Me, too. I really like this bartender. Not only is he a cutie, but he doesn't skimp on the liquor."

Rebecca gulped back her frustration before pulling her off the barstool.

"Where are we going?"

"Let's dance." She pushed her sister onto the dance floor with an enthusiastic smile.

The music pumped again. Lucy became lost in its rhythm. After the third song, Lug appeared behind her sister. He was a handsome, hard body. Exactly Lucy's type and she was eating it up. Rebecca put some distance between herself and the couple, finding a partner to blend in with. After two songs, Rebecca looked out over the dance floor to check on Lucy and Lug. Her body went cold when Lucy's friend Doug appeared at the bar.

Shit!

Rebecca dislodged her partner and headed for the bar. Her mind was spinning faster than her feet. A few feet away, she put a smile on her face before throwing herself forward, falling against him. She felt his arm around her and straightened out with a tipsy giggle. She looked at him with her best drunken sway.

"Sorry . . . I just bought these . . . wait." He met her eyes. "I know you . . . you're . . . you're Doug!"

"And you are?"

"I'm Rebecca." She used his apparent confusion to her advantage, "It figures you wouldn't remember."

"I remember, I just —"

"No, no . . . you've already been nailed, buster." She giggled and then groaned before she leaned against the bar, strategically brushing herself against him. "You know I've had people . . . specifically men . . . call me school mar mish . . . ishy?"

"Really?"

"Yes! Can you believe that . . . shit." Rebecca continued to slur her words to keep his attention. She raised her leg across his crotch to rest against the stool on the other side. "Does this look school mar mish . . . to you?"

The move caught him off guard, but she followed with a hand on his chest. She locked his eyes and a smile began to pull at the corners of his pierced mouth.

"School would be the last thing I would think of looking at you."

His hand rested against her knee. Having gotten his undivided attention, she stole a glance at the dance floor, seeing Lug still working her sister out of her belly necklace.

"Wow, it is really hot in here. I could use a drink," she said, initiating his detachment from her leg to ask the bartender for some drinks. "So what exactly is going on between you and my sister, Dougie?"

"Does it matter?" His hand planted itself on her ass.

"I wouldn't want to tread on any toes, she is my sister."

"She's sweet but a man could always use a little variety."

Rebecca gave him a girly giggle before looking back to the dance floor. Lugow and Lucy were nowhere in sight.

Crap . . .

"Why don't we go somewhere a little more private?" He fingered the inside of her leg while motioning to the bartended for one of the infamous *private* couches.

"Actually, Doug, if you'll excuse me," she backed away from the bar. "I'll be right back. I want to freshen up a little." She couldn't move fast enough to get away from him, her body trembling in revulsion.

Jesus Christ, what the hell was she doing? She leaned against the wall, gasping for air, Reynolds' words echoing in her head.

She used it as an excuse to torture you, Beccs.

Knowing that it would keep everyone occupied for a while. I, of course, was more than happy to oblige.

The words re-ignited the fire in her heart, but hurt more than she wanted to admit. She remembered what brought her there in the first place and closed her eyes, desperate for strength. She took a deep breath and looked at her watch.

Twelve forty-five AM . . . it's almost over . . .

Twelve forty-five . . . it's almost over . . . forty-five minutes and she would be back in his arms.

"Everything's set up," Eric turned and saw one of the tech leads standing beside him.

"Good. Double check everything, I don't want any bugs. We're going to get one shot at this. Eric stepped out the back door of the bar. The smell of cigarette smoke hit him. He turned to see his father puffing on a cigarette. "I thought you quit?"

"You keep giving me reasons to start again."

"So you think I shouldn't have let her do this either?"

"I didn't say that. I agree with what you did, but that doesn't mean I'm not concerned about her." Harry took another drag of his cigarette.

"Do you have an extra one of those?"

"Sure." He handed Eric the open pack.

"Did I do the right thing by letting her—"

"Letting her," Harry scoffed. "Son, I'm sorry, but you don't *let* Rebecca do anything. She either decides to do something or she doesn't. You don't really have much of a say in the matter."

"Yeah, I guess you have a point." Eric smiled, his mind admiring her fiery nature. "I'm still not sure this was a good idea. I understand her need to face Lucy, but she's been through so much."

"She has, which is why it's even more important that she does this. I have a feeling that this isn't about what happened, Lucy or the locket. I think this is about Rebecca taking her life back."

"You don't sound as worried as you look, old man."

"Hey, I said I understood it. Not that I wasn't disturbed by it."

Eric's phone rang. "Stiles."

"I have the locket and we're on our way to the bar."

"You got it?" He was relieved to hear Lug's voice.

"Yeah."

"Is she okay?"

"Yeah."

Eric's stomach clenched. "What happened?"

"Let's just say, it's been a rough night."

Rebecca stepped out of the stall to wash her hands when she heard Lucy's voice.

"Where have you been?" Lucy threw her arms around her.

"I've been here. You looked like you were having a fine time without me."

Lucy hugged her, releasing a breath of relief.

"Did you get his number?"

"No, some idiot pushed his way in and he disappeared," she put out a pouting lip before fixing her hair. "You have to help me find him, Beccs. I think I'm in love."

"Well, you'd better put the hearts and flowers on hold because I think I saw Doug at the bar."

"What are you talking about?"

"I was talking to the bartender and I swear I saw your friend Doug ordering a drink."

"Did you say anything to him?"

"Heck no, that's all you. I've got my own problems." Rebecca pulled out her phone, looking at it in confusion. "Huh, that's weird."

"What?"

"Oh, nothing. I have a voicemail, but I swear I don't remember my phone ringing."

"It's loud in here, Beccs."

"That's what's weird. It's from like five o'clock." She rolled her eyes and pretended to listen to her voicemail. Still watching her sister, she prepared the appropriate shocked response just as Lucy turned.

"What is it? What's wrong?"

Rebecca grabbed her sister by the arm, leading her out of the bathroom.

"Beccs, what's your problem?"

"Did you use my card to buy two plane tickets today?"

"I . . . well . . ."

"Lucy . . ."

"Well yeah . . . I did . . . I just . . ."

"Why didn't you just tell me?"

"I didn't think . . . you would be okay with . . . it."

"Why not? If you needed a vacation, you should've just told me. I don't have any problem with that. Sweetheart, we're family. When are you going to learn to trust me? I'm your sister. I've got your back."

"I . . . I'm sorry, Beccs. I just didn't think you'd be into it. What with the stiff and the *life*."

"Oh please, blood is thicker than water, Lucy." Rebecca gave her a wide smile. "So where are you going and who are you going with?"

"Jamaica and I was going to go with Doug."

"Wow, I wish I could go with you." Rebecca led her back toward the bar, going past the *private couches*. "Lucy, there's Doug."

Rebecca met Doug's gaze with a seductive smile. Lucy waved to him and then ran up to meet him. His eyes remained on her and Rebecca watched him embrace Lucy when her phone buzzed.

Rebecca turned away, seeing a message waiting for her.

I got it.

Leave now.

L

Before she could even digest what it said, Lucy was on her, pulling her away from the bar.

"Beccs!"

"Lucy what's wrong?" Her sister's face was terror struck and pale.

"I need your help."

"What is it, sweetheart?"

"I need you to get me out of here now."

"Tell me what's wrong."

"We need to go." Lucy's gaze fell just behind Rebecca. She grabbed her hand and pulled her toward the door. Within a few steps, the rush turned into a run. They burst out of the club into the night air. They kept their hands together as they raced through the parking lot.

Rebecca turned, seeing Doug just behind them.

Lugow had to be around somewhere. He wouldn't have left without her.

They reached the car and Lucy whined in fear as Rebecca unlocked the doors. They got in the car, but Lucy wasn't fast enough. Rebecca saw the passenger door open and her sister yanked from the car by her hair. Doug pulled her away from the car. He slammed her against a different car. Rebecca started her car and put it in reverse. She pulled out of the parking spot, turned the car and put it in park. She dislodged the tire iron from beneath her seat and got out to help her sister.

Doug's hand wrapped around Lucy's neck. Rebecca shoved the heel of her boot into the side of his knee. He stepped back and faced her. She used the tire iron like a baseball bat and swung. He released Lucy and deflected the blow with his shoulder. He lunged for her and tackled her to the ground.

He crushed her as she hit concrete. There were stars. She felt him rise and commanded her body to move. She thrust her hands against his chest, trying to shove him off. Rebecca heard him grunt.

Lucy jumped on his back and began pounding at his head. He shifted in an attempt to throw Lucy off.

Rebecca bent her knee and shoved him away.

He fell off and she got to her feet. She kicked him in the face while Lucy struggled to get out from beneath him. Rebecca moved to kick him again and he grabbed her boot. He swept her to the ground and once again, she landed hard, this time the fuzziness lasting a little longer.

A grunt followed, arms picking her up. Rebecca opened her eyes.

Lug was handling the man.

Lucy pulled her to her feet. Rebecca got her legs beneath her. Her mind was still a little dazed. She heard Lucy yell and she looked to Lug.

"Get out of here!

Rebecca took a breath, turned to the car and got in. She gulped back the bile in her throat and sped out of the parking lot.

"What the hell is going on?" She did her best to keep the charade going.

"Beccs, I'm sorry I just—"

"Listen to me, darlin', the only way I can have your back is if you tell me what's going on," Rebecca said. "The Rustic is a few miles from here. I don't know about you, but I could use a drink and an ice pack. So think about it and we can talk once our hearts stop racing, okay?"

Rebecca looked to Lucy who nodded, wiping tears from

her cheek. The rest of the drive was silent. Rebecca caught her breath, ignoring the ebbing pain at the back of her head.

One twenty-one AM.

Rebecca parked the car and the pair of them got out. She pulled on the door of the Rustic and felt like she was coming home. She knew everything around her was an illusion. She led Lucy to the bar and they took a seat in the corner.

Rebecca ordered them two shots as Lucy looked around.

"What's wrong?"

"I just don't feel right being here. This is Charlie's place and he's Eric's brother. Won't they be pissed when they find out about—"

"No, because they're never going to know. I don't tell Eric everything, Lucy."

"Yeah, right."

"You don't believe me?"

"Nope."

"Fine, I'll prove it."

"How?"

"I'll tell you something that I've never told Eric."

"Oh, this should be good."

"When Eric got hurt at the airport," Rebecca focused her rising emotions into the bottom of her glass. "There was a man. One of Marco's thugs. He tried to get me to leave with him. He called me a whore and threatened me and Eric."

"What happened?"

"I refused to leave, so he picked me up off the ground and started to drag me away." Rebecca took a visibly deep breath, wondering if he was listening. "I fought him and I was able to break free, but he came back. I panicked. I picked up Eric's gun and I shot him square in the chest."

"No, you—"

"Yeah, I did."

"Do the police know? Are you going to be in trouble?"

"It's all in my statement." She gulped back the second shot. "Adam said that it was self-defense and I have nothing to worry about."

"But you haven't told Eric?"

"Not yet."

"Is there anything else you haven't told him?"

"It doesn't matter," she wanted to change the subject before she lost control. "The point is, while this is Charlie's place, I know for a fact that he's off tonight and Eric's at the station. So there's nothing to worry about. Whatever you tell me is between us, I promise."

"Beccs . . ."

"Blood's thicker than water, remember?" Rebecca locked her sister's eyes.

"I . . . I did something."

"Okay."

"I stole something. Well, I didn't steal it. Someone else stole it and gave it to me to hold. It's beyond valuable and now I think I lost it."

"What do you mean you lost it? What are we talking about exactly?"

"The locket."

"Mom's locket?"

"It's a chip and I hid it in Mom's locket for safe keeping. It has information that's worth a lot and I mean *a lot* of money. To make a long story short, I took it from the hospital and we were going to Jamaica to sell it, but now it's gone."

"We as in you and Doug?"

"Yeah."

"Is Doug the one who gave it to you?"

"No, some guy, his name is George. He was the one who smuggled out the info to Doug and attached it to the locket."

"What's on it?"

"I don't know."

"Lucy, come on, you have to have some idea—"

"Okay fine, it's got the names of all the operations, handlers and agents the DOD are currently running abroad."

"Oh my God, Lucy, that's treason!"

"I swear I didn't know what was on it until last week when Doug told me! Beccs, I just want to be rid of the thing and now I've lost it and Doug's gonna—"

"How could you lose it?"

"I don't know, one minute I had it on me and the next I . . ."

The door opened and Doug stomped into the bar.

"You're late." Lucy's entire demeanor changed as she rose from her seat and faced him.

"What?" Rebecca should have been expecting it, but her stomach turned nonetheless.

"We don't have a lot of time—"

"Where is it?" Fire was in his eyes.

"Beccs has it, baby. She's gonna take us to it."

"Lucy, stop. What are you doing?"

"Shut up, Beccs, you're such an idiot."

Rebecca smacked her sister hard across the face.

"Bitch!" Lucy shouted.

"Oh, we're just getting started, little sister."

So far so good. Rebecca had gotten her in the door and now she just needed to bear her soul. Eric sat in the van parked at the back of the bar, watching the scene play out before him.

"Hey, how's it going?" Lug stepped into the van.

"So far so good."

"You got it?"

"Of course." He pulled a small baggy from his pocket, showing it to Eric.

"Okay put it somewhere safe, the last thing we need to do is lose it."

"Are we on track?"

"Looks like it." Lug took off his jacket and his focus went back to the conversation at the bar.

They listened as Lucy confessed to the theft.

"Here we go, let's get everybody in position," Eric said as he put in his earpiece and Lug took control of the van. Eric got out and headed to the back door. Opening it, he crept in, the noise from the bar hiding his entrance. Eric slid forward, trying to get a look at Rebecca.

Eric listened as the man demanded to know where it was. He motioned for his men to get ready to move before he began to venture into the main bar. All of the patrons were cops, so they were secure, but he wasn't taking any chances.

Lucy's voice was followed by a loud slap.

"Is there a problem here?" Eric said, successfully announcing his presence across the room.

"No, I think we just came to an understanding," Rebecca's voice was fierce and lined in blunt hostility.

"Beccs—"

"Shut up!" Her tone shut her sister down.

Doug decided he was going to get serious as he went for his weapon. Every patron in the bar was on his or her feet, guns pointed at him before he could twitch.

"Not the best idea there, Doug," Eric walked to the bar in a steady stroll.

"What's going on? Beccs, I—"

"It's over, Lucy." Rebecca's gaze remained steady and lethal. "We know everything and I mean everything."

"I don't—"

"We know about the locket, the stalking, Marco, Jorge, everything," she said, taking a step closer to her sister with each statement. Rebecca locked her fury-filled eyes as her sister's little world unraveled.

"Okay, let's wrap this up." On Eric's command, the cluster of patrons took Lucy and Doug into custody.

"Beccs, let me explain, It's not my fault. I need you, please! Beccs, I love you, you're my sister!"

Rebecca turned away.

Eric placed a reassuring hand on the small of her back.

"Rebecca listen to me, please! I'm sorry . . . please, Beccs, I'm so sorry—"

"I can't do it anymore, Lucy. I'm sorry," Rebecca met her sister's eyes, her voice breaking with emotion. "It's too much, you've gone too far and I can't forgive you anymore."

"Fine, you fucking bitch! I knew I couldn't count on you . . . I knew it was all a lie! I should've just had Marco kill you instead of sell you!" Lucy fought against the officers.

Eric waved them to take her away. "Why don't you go to the office, I'll be there in a minute."

Rebecca nodded and walked toward the back of the bar.

"You had your perfect fucking life and I took it away, didn't I? I took it all, even your baby! It's the only thing I did right, protecting that baby from having you as its mother!"

Eric's chest went hard as he looked to Lucy and then saw Rebecca turn to look at her sister. She didn't say anything, just met her eyes before she walked away.

"Get her out of here already!" Eric followed them out the front door before signing them over and watching them go. He let it all roll off his back. He walked back into the bar and saw both Rebecca and Lugow at separate tables, giving their statements. The teams began breaking down the set up and Eric sent a majority of them back to the station with a nod of thanks.

He went back to the surveillance van to confirm they had

everything they needed. Watching the recording from start to finish didn't desensitize the impact of what happened. If anything, it twisted the knife in even further.

Once Lucy and Doug were taken into custody, everything came out. It was revealed that they'd been playing Marco for months. When Rebecca came for Lucy, it was Doug who found her first and came up with the initial plan. They knew Rebecca had the locket. So the stalking began, giving Marco no way to approach Rebecca without being exposed. Doug was the one who convinced Marco to send Jorge to Vegas in the hope that Jorge would be Jorge and buy them some time.

Lucy then directed Jorge's activities through Doug. As Lucy became more unstable, the more she lost control, leaving Jorge to his own psychotic devices. Once Jorge was caught, Marco arrived to retrieve the locket. Lucy used it as a means of escape and played along, biding her time until the locket fell into her hands at the hospital.

"How did it go?" Charlie asked as he walked up to stand beside his brother in the back of the bar.

"It's over."

"She confessed?"

"Pretty much. We got the locket back, we know what's on it and we know what they were going to do with it." Eric leaned against the wall, his hands in his pockets.

"So she pulled it off."

"Was there ever any doubt?"

"Nah," Charlie replied with a shrug. "Well, maybe just a little, but don't tell her I said that."

"Ah, blackmail material."

"Is she okay?"

"Yeah, she's okay."

I refuse to be a weeping weak idiot, outside of right here . . .

Watching her talking to the reports officer, he ached to hold her. The need stabbed at him and he told his heart to be patient.

"How are you doing?"

"Fine, good, looking forward to some time off."

"You're actually going to take a vacation?"

"Yeah, I think we are." He mulled the possibility of taking her away from all of this for a while.

"I hope you do, you deserve it," Charlie squeezed Eric's shoulder before walking away.

The sun was beginning to crest the desert plain and he took a drag from his cigarette.

"Since when do you smoke?"

Eric pushed the hit out of his lungs and turned. Her hair glistened, capturing the small slivers of sunlight as they peaked over the horizon and a deep sigh washed over him

"I'm not sure," he replied with a smirk, unable to pull his eyes away. She removed the cigarette from his hand and took a drag. Handing it back to him, his arm wrapped around her as she rested her head on his shoulder. "You ready to go home?"

He felt her nod and he tossed the cigarette away. He opened the truck door and she climbed in. He walked around, got in and started the truck. She took hold of his arm, resting her cheek against him and closed her eyes.

It was after five when they walked into the house. They both headed to the bedroom in silence and changed before crawling into bed. He wrapped his arms around her and she curled against his chest. Safe in each other's arms they fell asleep.

Chapter Eleven

Eric shifted, feeling her warmth wrap around him, and he just laid there in the quiet haven of their bed. Listening to the steady rhythm of her breath, it lulled his relaxation and he didn't want to move.

His mind began to settle into itself and awaken. With it came all the images, words and emotion of recent events. His chest began to tug at him in concern as he wondered what was going to happen when she opened her eyes.

The only consolation was that it was over. The book closed and they could move on with their lives. He took a deep breath and opened his eyes to look at the clock. It was after one and he debated just closing his eyes again.

Eric felt her shift in his arms. He turned on his side, watching her beautiful face start to wake up. His fingers slid through her hair as her eyes opened. The amazing blue he craved and so needed to survive stared up at him. He continued to play with her hair and she smiled. "Hey, bright eyes."

"Hey, hero."

He leaned down, brushing a sweet kiss on her lips.

"What time is it?"

"A little after one." He continued to play with her hair and she stretched like a cat before rolling onto her side.

"Can we just stay in bed all day?"

"I'm liking the sound of that." He wrapped his arms around her waist and nibbled her neck. "We have nowhere to be."

"Yes, but unfortunately, I stink of smoke and booze which is gross. I'm going to jump in the shower." She gave him a quick kiss before rolling out of his arms. "Can you start some coffee?"

His stomach twisting, he bit his tongue when she left his side and disappeared into the bathroom. He got out of bed and started the coffee as requested. He decided to be patient and wait for the dam to break when she was ready. He pushed his hand through his hair and went to the fridge for cream. As he filled his coffee cup, Eric began toying with the notion of taking her away.

Going on a real vacation, complete with room service, clear water and white sandy beaches. He wondered if she would be open to the idea. There wasn't anything keeping her here now. She didn't have Lucy to worry about or take care of, although he figured it would be best if he didn't present it like that.

Glancing at the bedroom, he knew nothing was going to happen until she faced and accepted what Lucy had done. Until then, their lives were on indefinite hold. Picking up his phone, he checked his email while drinking his liquid fuel. He heard her padding out of the bedroom and looked up. Her hair was still wet and she hadn't gotten dressed. Wrapped in a thick white terry cloth robe, her milky legs peaked from beneath its folds as she approached. She was intoxicating.

She headed straight to the coffee pot when Eric's phone rang in his hand.

"Stiles."

"Hey, I was going to leave you a message. I figured you guys would still be asleep," Adam greeted.

"No rest for the weary, right? What's up?"

"I just wanted you to know that Lucy and Doug have been handed over to the NSA. They came and got them this morning and with the exception of some paperwork, we're done."

Eric half-heard the news as he watched Rebecca moved around the kitchen, randomly picking up, wiping down and shifting things as she went. His entire body bristled. He wanted her to just stop and breathe for a minute, but he remained silent. "That's great, thanks for the update."

"How's Rebecca?"

"She's good. We just got up, so I think we're both still a little foggy."

"Is she feeling okay?"

"Yeah, why?"

"Lug mentioned she hit her head pretty hard last night and I just wanted to make sure she's okay. And . . . she didn't tell you anything about this, so I'm going to shut up now."

"Yeah, thanks. I'll ask her and let you know," he replied in slight irritation before he ended the call.

"Was that Adam?"

"Yeah, he was asking how you are."

"Oh that's sweet of him."

Eric tugged at her hand, pulling her toward him before resting his hand on her hips. "Lug mentioned you hit your head last night?"

"Oh yeah, I forgot."

"What happened?"

"Doug decided to get a little physical when Lucy and I tried to leave the club."

"And?"

"And I kicked his ass." A broad grin spread over her face, making him laugh.

"You did, did you?"

"You can even ask Lug, he'll confirm my story."

"Yeah well, I think I'm going to be reminding Lug and

Adam just whose partners they are," Eric's hand moved up, massaging the back of her neck. "So you're okay?"

"I'm fine, not even a headache."

He leaned forward, kissing her forehead. "Okay, I'm going to jump in the shower."

"Have fun."

The hesitation at leaving her alone curled in his stomach, but he pushed it away, not wanting to hover. Letting the heated water pour over him, he hadn't realized how much his body ached. *God, I really need a vacation.*

Eric dressed and walked into the kitchen half an hour later. He didn't see any sign of her until he heard the door to the garage closing.

"Where'd you go?"

"I was just taking out the garbage."

"Babe, I could've done that." He noticed she'd gotten dressed in a simple pair of jeans and a t-shirt.

"You were in the shower and I wanted to clean up." She walked past him to the washing machine. "Can you get the laundry out of the bathroom, please?"

"Sure." Eric went to the bathroom and began collecting the discarded articles of clothing. A crashing of glass erupted from the kitchen. Eric dropped the items in his hands and rushed out of the room. He found a pool of light brown liquid beneath the shattered pieces of a coffee cup, but she wasn't anywhere in sight.

"Rebecca," he called out and then heard a crash from the spare bedroom. He followed the noise and found her yanking Lucy's clothing out of the closet. "Beccs, what are you—"

"I don't want her here." Her voice was absent and broken.

He doubted she was even talking to him. She was trembling in anger and he watched her go to the dresser, ripping out the drawers and dumping them on the floor. Her arm then swept over the top, sending all the items crashing to the floor.

"I want her out."

"Beccs—" Her eyes were unfocused and Eric watched her emotions rising out of control. "Beccs, stop."

"No I want her gone!" She grabbed a vase off the bookshelves and sent it careening into the opposite wall where it shattered into pieces. Her eyes were a riveting dark blue as her body convulsed in rage.

He moved without thought, reaching her just as she yanked the bookcase off the wall. He encircled her arms and she fought against him, but he pulled her back and away from the falling bookcase as it crashed to the floor. "Beccs, stop." He held her tight. "Baby, please . . . please."

He heard her heavy breath shake and he loosened his grip as her body crumbled. Her legs collapsed and he cradled her as they eased down onto the floor.

"How could she . . . why . . ." She trembled.

His emotions got the better of him.

"I should've known . . . I could've . . ."

"No . . . what she did doesn't change anything. It's not your fault, there's nothing we could've done." Eric turned her into his chest.

The tears came hard and fast as she let go and they both cried.

He hadn't known what to expect or what was going to trigger it. Eric saw her hand gripping something soft and blue. He looked closer and realized what it was a baby hat. She must've found it when she was cleaning up and a wave of remorse swept through him. It didn't seem right that something so precious should invoke such agony.

He caressed her hair as she clung to him. He realized it didn't matter what the trigger was, it happened and now they could deal with it.

She seemed to relax a little. He glanced down at her tear-stained cheeks, the look of anguish and exhaustion unmistakable. He shifted, her head resting on his shoulder.

"I thought I'd returned everything." Rebecca smoothed the blue baby hat beneath her fingers. "I found the two bags in front of her room with a note asking me to return . . . that's where I started to figure it out. In the middle of Baby Emporium explaining the reason for my return."

"Sweetheart . . ." His heart ached in regret and he kissed her forehead.

"How could she . . ." The reality hit her again and she curled around him.

He scooped her into his arms and carried her into their bedroom. Kneeling on the bed, he laid her down with him, never breaking their embrace.

Still safe within his arms, Eric gazed down into her tear-filled eyes. Her fingertip lined his jaw before wiping away his tears. He could feel their joined breath and beating hearts as his hand wrapped in her hair. He kissed her forehead, the tears on her cheeks, the tip of her nose and then her soft lips. She melted beneath him and he pulled her closer as the relief, sorrow and love hit them all at once.

Eric felt her fingers curl into his hair and their mutual need rose. Their breath and tongues spoke a language all their own. He could feel his entire being screaming for her. Before he got swept away, he pulled back, catching his breath as he looked down into her eyes.

"I love you so much."

Her hand caressed his cheek and she looked at him with loving eyes.

"I'm tired of feeling broken. I don't want to feel like this anymore." She lifted her head off the pillow and pressed her open lips to his.

He could feel her tender wanting as he relinquished control to his heart. Her kisses were soft, deep and slow, feeding the growing pressure in his body.

He was terrified to release his locked embrace around her and while he knew it was irrational, she didn't seem to mind. If anything, she insisted, pulling him back anytime the distance between them became too great.

He lined a trail of kisses down her neck, relishing the smell of her hair and the sweet taste of her skin. He could feel her fingers tracing up the sides of his ribs and he squirmed beneath her touch. She tugged at his shirt and he yanked it over his head. Her mouth attached to his chest and, closing his eyes in an attempt of restraint, he felt her mouth hit his collarbone. He took the opportunity to go back to her neck.

He rolled onto his side, his arms still wrapped around her body. She continued to plant sweet kisses along his neck. His hands pulled her against him while sliding up the soft curves of her back.

He was so elated just to have her against him, he thought he would explode. He reached out, cupping her cheek, pulling her to his lips. Her body rested against his chest. She kissed and pulled at his mouth with a desperate need.

He pulled her shirt up and over her head before unclasping and discarding her bra. He rolled her on top of him.

Her legs straddled him, her hair raining down around him. She covered his body in kisses while her hands pulled at his pants. She undid his button and zipper and her warm hand wrapped around his cock.

Unexpectedly, her absence from his embrace was too much. He sat up, his arm resting on her lower back while his free hand tangled itself in her hair, cradling the back of her neck. He saw her look of surprise before he claimed her soft mouth.

She melted against him and he rolled her beneath him. She met the fervor of his kiss and continued to push him free of his pants.

After a few moments and a fit of giggles, he kicked them off his legs as her nails pulled up along his back, sending chills through his entire body.

His tongue twisted at the nape of her neck and he nipped at the sensitive skin with his teeth. He targeted the spot just behind her ear that he knew made her moan. He received the expected response and lingered there a moment in torture. Her nails dug into his ribs and he moved down her neck to her collarbone. His thumb rolled a nipple beneath it before his mouth latched onto the other. He nipped at it, hearing her gasp before he rolled his tongue, feeling it harden between his lips. He released it and gave the opposite nipple a small pinch before sucking it between his lips. He flicked his tongue in a relentless pattern until he heard a low moan emanate from her chest. He moved over her body, his intent to erase any thought she had outside of their lovemaking.

He resumed his earlier crusade to kiss every bruise on her magnificent body. He tugged her jeans down her hips and legs, planting a kiss on each space of skin he revealed. He discarded her pants and her breath came in shivers and gasps. His mouth explored her thighs and moved up while his hands wrapped around her slim hips and pulled off the last piece of lace covering her body.

His breath teased her center and her body arched. His tongue was waiting and he worshipped her clit with long torturous strokes. Her body writhed. His teasing ignited waves through her and she pushed against his mouth. His own restraint began to collapse as his cock hardened.

"Eric . . ."

He heard her call to him in breathless wanting and, discarding what was left of his clothing, he crawled up her body, planting kisses and nips along the way.

He rested his body against hers, his mouth descending. It captured her lips, expressing all the desires pouring from his body. His arm wrapped around her waist before he rolled onto his back, taking her with him.

Her lips still attached to his, she wiggled her hips and trapped his cock against the folds of her pussy. She pushed her pelvis against his shaft and began to stroke him with her body. She nibbled on his chest, her nails running down his sides as she continued to move against his body. His hips instinctively thrust against her, his cock hardening with every caress of her body. She made a subtle shift and with his next movement, he impaled her. His cock spasmed in delight, pushing a moan from both of them. Her arms resting on either side of his head, she showered him with deep, longing kisses. His hands wrapped in her luxurious hair as she began to move.

Her hips rolled against him, sending sparks through his groin, into the berth of his cock. Her movements were slow and steady and his hands kneaded her shoulders and back. She lifted herself, straightening her back and the pressure increased within him. His hands went to her hips, guiding her as she moved up and down. His pelvis rose to meet her movement, deepening his strokes within her pussy. He watched her body as it glistened with sweat and moved like liquid over him. Her head fell back with a deep groan before she leaned forward, resting her hands on his chest. She reached for him, kissing him, and he caught her breasts in his hands. He began playing with her nipples and she shuddered as she continued to move.

"Eric . . ." she gasped and he lifted his pelvis.

In an unbroken siege on her mouth, Eric rolled her beneath him. His cock still embedded within her, he could feel her body breathe around him. He reveled in the closeness as he swam in her eyes, his fingers caressing her cheek.

Her hips twisted beneath him and he groaned in pleasure as she trailed her fingertips up and down his body. He pulled out of her and then plunged forward, a gasp of delight escaping her lips. He extended the delightfully slow torture, repeating his cock's stroking of her body. She coiled and curved against his deep, deliberate thrusts. His pace quickened with her breath as they drove to quench their steady but urgent need for release.

He felt her cunt close around him, squeezing him within her body and his cock tightened. The passion between them exploded, leaving them both trembling and overcome with love.

Eric stared down into her liquid-filled eyes as he kissed her, drops of wetness sliding down their cheeks and in that perfect moment, they began to heal.

Her senses awakened to soft, tender kisses on her neck and his warmth around her body. She smiled and purred. His touch ran over her like water and she tugged his arm around her a little closer.

"I love you, Rebecca," he said into her hair.

She couldn't help but smile as she turned to kiss him. He leaned forward, caressing her lips. "I love you, too."

Eric broke the kiss, idly playing with her hair and she found herself staring at him.

"Whatcha thinking about, bright eyes?"

"Everything I haven't told you." Rebecca watched his eyes for some kind of reaction. Instead, he caressed her cheek and kissed her forehead.

"You don't have to tell me anything you don't want to," he looked down with concerned, honest eyes. "You know that, don't you?"

"Eric . . ."

"Listen to me." An edge of sternness tinted his voice. "Whether you tell me or not isn't going to change anything. I want you to tell me if and when you're ready, not because you think you have to, okay?"

She nodded in understanding. His statement, while wonderful and understanding, didn't, however, change her mind. She wanted it all out in the open, if for no other reason than to just let it go. She was tired of carrying it all and maybe if she told him, it would start to go away. The only problem now was that she wasn't sure where to start. "Did you hear any of my conversation with Lucy at the bar?"

"Some of it, why?"

"She asked me to prove that I don't tell you everything." She grabbed his shirt, pulling it over her head, and sat up in bed. "So I had to come up with an example."

"Beccs, you—"

"You were bleeding and I was freaking out." Rebecca rose up out of the bed, the entire scenario replaying in her mind. "He came out of nowhere and . . . he demanded that I get up. I told him no, but he . . . he wouldn't listen. He grabbed me by the waist and lifted me away from you. I squirmed and managed to break free, but he wouldn't—"

"Rebecca."

She turned to find him standing just behind her. She had turned into his chest and she looked up at him. "I shot him." She watched him in fear. His expression didn't change and she panicked. Her eyes started to tear and her body shook. "When he pulled me away, I saw your gun on the ground. I just grabbed it. The next thing I knew . . ."

"Okay, it's okay." He pulled her into him. "You did what you had to do, sweetheart. I just wish you would have told me."

"I'm sorry . . . I didn't . . ."

"Does anyone else know?"

"It's in my statement, so I would assume Lugow knows. Adam said that it was a clear case of self-defense and that I shouldn't worry about it," she replied as she looked up at him in worry. "Is that right? Eric, I didn't . . ."

"It's fine. You're fine. Adam is right and there is nothing for you to worry about, okay?" He wrapped his arms around her and she hid herself in his embrace.

"I feel like I'm falling apart. Nothing makes sense . . . and I . . ." She cried into his chest. "I don't know what to do."

"Hey," he pulled her back to the bed. He sat down and pulled her onto his lap as he threaded his fingers into her hair. "You're my tough-as-nails redhead remember? We are going to get through this, Beccs, okay?"

She nodded again, resting her head on his shoulder.

"So, I was thinking," he pulled her closer, his fingertips lining her back. "What do you think about us getting out of here for a while?"

"A vacation?"

"Yeah, I was already planning to take some time off," he said with a smile as he played with her hair. "I'm sure we can convince your job to let you go for at least a little while."

"Really?"

He nodded.

She could see the excitement in his eyes. "Where would we go?"

"I'm thinking somewhere warm, with clear waters and sandy beaches."

"Do you think we can get away?"

"If that's what you want, I'll make it happen." He kissed her.

A genuine sense of delight spread over her, making her smile.

"Okay, I know that you're amazing, but how, exactly, did you pull this off?" Rebecca's head rested on his shoulder.

"Pull what off?"

"Are you kidding me?" Her mock disbelief was clear. "Not only did we go on an unforgettable vacation in Cabo, but you got a Leer Jet to bring us home?"

"Nothing's too good for my redhead," he said, smiling before he kissed her.

Once everything was out in the open, charges were brought against Lucy and Doug. Rebecca walked away with Eric's support. Her sister needed to face the consequences alone. As soon as they weren't needed, Eric booked the next flight out of town.

They'd spent two full weeks in Cabo San Lucas. He'd pulled some strings, got them a suite and there was no looking back. It was just what they needed and by the end of the first week, he saw the first signs of the sparkle returning to her eyes. Once he got her to relax, the rest was easy and they enjoyed the scenery as well as just being together.

It was incredible to watch her come alive again. He learned so much about her and fell even more in love with her.

"Thank you."

"For what?" he asked as she kissed him.

"For being wonderful."

"I'm just glad to see you smile," he replied before the phone rang. "Hello?"

"Mr. Stiles, this is the captain. We are getting ready to land."

"Thanks."

"Was that the captain?"

"Yeah, we're about to land."

"Already?" Disappointment filled her eyes. "I guess it had to end."

He suppressed a small grin beneath the tightening of his stomach and twenty minutes later, the plane landed. Their luggage was unloaded and Eric led her down the stairs and into a black sedan.

"Eric, what's going on?"

"Ah, nothing. I just didn't want to bother anyone to come and get us," he replied. "And . . . if no one knows we're here, then they will leave us alone for a few more days."

"Wow, you are devious," she said with a grin as he played with her lips.

"You have no idea," he said as he continued to occupy her with succulent kisses. It took a moment for them to realize that the car had stopped.

"Did the car stop?"

"I think so."

"We can't be home yet." The window between them and the driver slid open.

"You said you wanted to stop for coffee, sir?"

"Oh yeah, I forgot."

Rebecca looked at him in bewilderment. "Coffee?"

"Yeah, it's still early and it's on the way." He opened the door and got out, watching as she exited the car next to him.

"When did you tell the driver . . ." it took a moment before she noticed their surroundings and her eyes went wide as she looked to him. "Eric, what . . ."

"I wanted some coffee," he said with a huge grin as she started to laugh.

"Are you crazy?"

"About you." He pulled her close as she continued to look at him in shock. "So do you want some coffee or not?"

"Definitely,"

He took her hand and they walked into the Dallas coffee house where they'd had their first quasi-date. She was grinning ear to ear as they ordered coffee and she laughed aloud when she saw the reserved sign on the table where they'd sat so many months before.

"I can't believe you did this."

"Why?" he replied with a grin. "Have jet will travel. When are we going to get another chance to come back here?"

"I love you, Eric Stiles," she said as she leaned forward and kissed him. "So, should we play our game again?"

"Why not, you go first."

"First thing you're going to do when we get home?"

"Kiss you and convince you to take a shower with me. Favorite time of day?"

"Falling asleep with you. Least favorite time of day?"

"Leaving you . . . anytime. Most annoying habit?"

"Mine or yours?"

"Mine."

"Your inability to pick up your clothes. Most annoying habit?"

"Your inability to not clean," he replied with a smirk and she blushed. "Favorite body part?"

"Your arms. Now you?"

"Your eyes. Last time we were here . . . did you see me watch you kick that guy's ass at pool?"

"Yes. What were you thinking?"

"That I'd never seen such beautiful blue eyes in my entire life. What were you thinking when I came around the corner in the hallway at the hotel?"

"That my wish had been granted. How about you?"

"That if I didn't kiss you, I was going to die. Why did you leave?"

She looked thoughtfully down at her coffee. "When I woke up, you were so peaceful and the thought of saying goodbye to you hurt too much. So, I decided it would be better if I just left things as they were. Keeping the perfect memory intact."

The admission tugged at him. Eric took a breath and pulled a piece of paper out of his wallet, laying it in front of her.

She looked at him in confusion before opening it.

Stunned, her eyes moist with emotion, she got up and took a seat in his lap, wrapping her arms around his neck.

"I can't believe you kept it."

"Of course, I kept it. It was the only piece of you I had left."

His hand on her cheek, she pressed her forehead to his. He lifted his lips to caress hers, his heart overflowing in devotion. He held her close and the embrace ended as they smiled at each other.

"I have an idea." Her eyes glowed. "How about you and I go make some spending money?"

"Why? Do you need some new shoes?"

Her eyes widened as she laughed. "As a matter of fact I do. You've been talking to Donna."

"A little," he brushed her hair over her shoulder. "And how do you propose we do this?"

"Well, I was thinking maybe you could teach me how to play pool . . ."

Finishing their coffee, they worked out how they were going to pull off their little hustle and headed over to the hotel bar. Walking in, they played the happy couple, had a few drinks and hit the pool tables. Rebecca played a very convincing giggling girl as she tried to pay attention to her boyfriend showing her how to play pool. After two fake games, a man approached, looking for a game. Eric said he'd be interested in playing and proceeded to keep the game close even though he lost. Rebecca then chimed in that she wanted to play and batting her blue eyes, he was convinced.

Eric watched her reel the poor sucker in as she played the

part to the hilt. She got him to keep raising the bet and she began to win, making it look like luck. This irritated her opponent and he had the need to recover his male ego. It was then that the magic happened. Within one game, she got him to triple his bet, lose and still challenge her to a rematch. The crowd began to gather and she swept the floor with him.

This, of course, spawned a rally of challengers who all proceeded to lose to her skill and Eric joined the party when they played pairs in their opponents' attempt to find a chink in their armor. They walked away from the table with eight hundred dollars and went to the bar for a drink.

"That was way too easy," he whispered into her ear as their beers arrived. "You have no idea how much I want you right now."

"Well we are in a hotel." She grabbed the loops of his jeans and pulled him closer.

"Oh yeah." He kissed her while digging in his back pocket and then held the key up for her to see. She smiled and, finishing their beers, they left the bar and headed for the elevator.

As soon as the elevator doors closed, she jumped into his arms, wrapping her legs around his waist, devouring his mouth. The doors opened and distracted by her insistent lips, he forgot where he was going.

She laughed at him, released her legs and landed on the floor in front of him. Kissing him again, she slipped her hand into his pocket and grabbed the key. He watched her look at the room number with a smile as she led him down the hall. He stopped and waited for her to notice.

"Eric . . ." Rebecca turned to see him waiting. "What are you doing?"

"I was trying to figure out the moment it happened."

"What happened?"

"The moment I fell in love with you," Eric looked down

into her eyes, his fingertips tracing her lips. "It was right here, the first time I kissed you."

"Eric . . ."

"Rebecca, I want to wake up and see your beautiful eyes every day for the rest of my life. You changed me and everything I thought I wanted for the future. My future is with you, I'm hopelessly devoted to you and I can only hope that you'll have me." He stepped back and got down on one knee. Looking up at her, he could see her eyes widen in astonishment. "Marry me, Beccs, I love you and my life means nothing if you're not in it."

Tears poured from her eyes as her hand covered her mouth in disbelief. He pulled out the small box he'd been carrying around for three weeks. He opened it, but her eyes never left his and his heart soared. Her hand was still covering her mouth as she cried. His heart skipped when she didn't say anything and just stood staring at him. He waited, her eyes glowing before she dropped her hand, revealing her beautiful smile, and she nodded.

"Yes . . . yes!"

Eric heard the words, jumped to his feet and pulled her into his arms. He kissed her before lifting her off her feet and twirling her around in happiness. He stopped, looking into the eyes that saved him. She smiled up at him, a few stray tears sliding down her cheek.

He kissed her again and then remembered the ring in his hand. He pulled the ring from the box to show her.

She looked at it. "Oh, Eric, it's perfect."

"May I?" He took her warm hand in his as he slipped the ring on her finger. It fit and he smiled as he watched her look down at her hand.

"It's so beautiful."

"You're beautiful." He wrapped his hands in her hair, losing himself in her electric eyes, before he met her lips with a deep, soulful kiss. Her arms wrapped around his neck and his hands encompassed her waist, lifting her against him. She once again looped her legs around his waist.

"So, what's our room number again?"

"Room three forty-eight."

She kissed him again as he carried her down the hall toward the room.

"Make love to me like you did that first night."

"For the rest of your life."

About the Author

As a wife, mother of three, full time corporate employee, and novelist I have little time to do anything not focused. Having written for most of my life, my writing heart beats to the fast paced, twisting, romantic thriller.

Amy works for a global document solutions company and current resides in Texas.

I believe Everything Happens for a Reason

I believe in True Love

I believe in Fate

I believe in Optimism

I believe in Imagination

I believe in Hard Work

I believe in Family

www.ingramcontent.com/pod-product-compliance
Lightning Source LLC
Chambersburg PA
CBHW061519050726
47593CB00002B/638